Ari tore his mouth away and looked down at her, at their bodies still plastered together.

'You're so beautiful. Why do you hide yourself away, Lucy?'

His words broke her out of this sensual stasis: *so beautiful...* She wasn't beautiful. She'd heard those words a million times before. Not directed at her—never at her. But at someone else. Someone who had craved them; someone who had spent her life being defined by men's opinion of her.

The shock of everything suddenly hit, and made Lucy jerk back violently, knocking his hand away and pulling her dress together again. She had a mortifying image in her head of wantonly pressing as close as she could, and the shame of her reaction to that made her feel nauseous.

Her voice was shaking and thin, too high. 'This is completely inappropriate. I'm your *assistant*.'

Abby Green got hooked on Mills & Boon® romances while still in her teens, when she stumbled across one belonging to her grandmother in the west of Ireland. After many years of reading them voraciously, she sat down one day and gave it a go herself. Happily, after a few failed attempts, Mills & Boon bought her first manuscript.

Abby works freelance in the film and TV industry, but thankfully the four a.m. starts and the stresses of dealing with recalcitrant actors are becoming more and more infrequent, leaving her more time to write!

She loves to hear from readers, and you can contact her through her website at www.abby-green.com She lives and works in Dublin.

RUTHLESS GREEK BOSS, SECRETARY MISTRESS

BY
ABBY GREEN

First published in Great Britain 2009
Harlequin Mills & Boon Limited,
Eton House, 18-24 Paradise Road, Richmond, Surrey TW9 1SR

© Abby Green 2009

ISBN: 978 0 263 87458 7

Set in Times Roman 10½ on 12 pt
01-1209-55921

Harlequin Mills & Boon policy is to use papers that are natural, renewable and recyclable products and made from wood grown in sustainable forests. The logging and manufacturing process conform to the legal environmental regulations of the country of origin.

Printed and bound in Spain
by Litografia Rosés, S.A., Barcelona

RUTHLESS GREEK BOSS, SECRETARY MISTRESS

This is for Ann and Iona—getting to number ten wouldn't have been half the amazing journey it's been without either one of you by my side. I'm indebted to both of you wonderful ladies and writers, and am looking forward to all of our shared experiences to come! With much thanks and love, for everything.

CHAPTER ONE

'YOU'RE the coldest man I ever met. If you have a heart it's made of stone. You're cruel and contemptible. I *hate* you.' The woman's strident voice quivered dangerously on the last word and came through the heavy oak door with effortless ease.

There was silence, and then the ominously low rumble of a man's voice. Short, sharp, succinct. Lucy could imagine only too well the glacial look that was most likely accompanying those indistinct words. She sighed as she heard the woman splutter indignantly, but then she was off again, her voice rising so high now that Lucy feared for the crystal decanter on the drinks board nearby. While Lucy was new to these scenes first-hand, she had to reflect that the rumours she'd heard over the past two years hadn't been a myth after all. The voice was drawing her attention back to the present moment.

'*Don't think that you can seduce your way back into my bed after treating me like this!*'

Lucy had just enough time for a cynical smile as she reflected that if her new boss was to so much as arch an eyebrow this woman would undoubtedly be back in his bed in a heartbeat before the door was suddenly flung open. She looked studiously at her computer screen, trying to sink down in her seat and be as unobtrusive as possible.

Being unobtrusive was her trademark: it was what had got her this coveted job, along with her impeccable credentials and references. There was a lull, a pseudo-calm in the middle of the storm. Lucy didn't look up, but could visualise the woman standing dramatically on the threshold of the palatial office. Tall, sleek and blonde. Stunningly beautiful, from the top of her shiny head to the tip of her expensively manicured toes, evident through the peepholes of a pair of sky-high heels. She was reputedly one of the most alluring women in the world, but apparently hadn't managed to hold his attention for longer than a few weeks.

'Needless to say you won't be hearing from me again.'

The door slammed shut with such violence that Lucy winced. He wouldn't appreciate that. Even though Lucy had only been working for him for two months she already knew that he hated scenes. A cloud of noxious perfume lingered in the wake of the tall woman's exit. She hadn't even glanced Lucy's way.

Lucy breathed a sigh of relief and then heard a loud thump, as if a fist was connecting with a hard surface. She counted to ten, and on the count of ten the door opened. She looked up and willed any emotion or reaction from her face. Her boss stood there, filling the frame easily. Veritable sparks of energy crackled from his body.

Aristotle Levakis, CEO of Levakis Enterprises which encompassed all aspects of a dizzyingly successful global imports and exports business.

Tall, broad-shouldered, lean hipped. Every hard-muscled, dark olive-skinned inch of him adding up to a—currently bristling—Greek alpha male in his potent and virile prime.

His distinctive light green eyes skewered Lucy to the spot, almost as if the last ten minutes had been *her* fault. Instantly she felt breathless; her heart hammered. She hated that she was aware of him. But the best part of two years spent viewing

him from a distance, along with every other ogling female in
his thousand-employee-strong company, had done little to
help diminish the devastating impact of working in such close
proximity to him. A memory surfaced and familiar heat
flooded her. If only she *had* been kept at a safe distance he
might not be having this effect on her now—but there had
been that moment in a lift, almost a year ago…Lucy ruthlessly
crushed that memory stone-dead. Now was *not* the time.

But, much to her chagrin and dismay, she couldn't halt her
reaction. It was something about the way he'd obviously just
raked a hand through his unruly ink-black hair, leaving it
even more dishevelled, and the way his jaw was so defined
and hard it looked as if it was hewn from granite. His cheekbones and that full lower lip softened the hard edges, giving
him the look of a master of sensuality—which by all accounts
he was. Yet dark brows drawn together over those deep-set,
amazing eyes took away any lingering pretty edges.

'Lucy,' he rapped out, distaste for the recent dramatics
etched all over his handsome face. 'Get in here. *Now.*'

Lucy blinked and landed back to earth with a bump. What
was she doing? Sitting here mentally listing her boss's attri-
butes as if he wasn't standing there looking at her as if he
wanted to throttle someone. Caught short, which she never
was, she scrambled up somewhat inelegantly from her chair
and walked towards him, but then, to add insult to injury, she
dropped her pad and pen from suddenly nerveless fingers. She
bent down to pick them up, cursing herself in her head, *and*
cursing the fact that her skirt was too tight when it resisted
her movement. She'd put it in the wrong wash and it had
shrunk about two sizes; with no time to shop for a replace-
ment it had had to do, but now she was terrified it might split
at the seams. The thought of that made her go hot all over.

If Aristotle Levakis so much as guessed for a second that
he had any effect on her she'd be out on her ear and replaced

so fast her head would be spinning. She didn't have to remind herself that was exactly what had happened to his last two unfortunate assistants.

Speed had been of the essence as his in-house headhunters had scrambled to find the next best person. Lucy had since discovered that Levakis Enterprises was involved in a top secret series of merger meetings, and the luxury of extending the search to outside the company hadn't been an option.

As luck would have had it, Lucy's boss, Levakis' senior legal counsel, had retired the very day of the last unfortunate PA's demise. Lucy had been vetted and promoted within twenty-four hours to the most terrifying and yet exciting position of her career so far: Levakis' personal secretary, heading up a team of five junior administrative assistants, not to mention staff in Athens and New York.

When she straightened up, taking care to breathe in, all this raced through her brain and she felt thoroughly flustered. She pushed her glasses higher on her nose and felt her cheeks grow even hotter. Aristotle moved back to let her precede him into his office, and she caught the look of exasperation that crossed his face as he articulated her own thoughts out loud with narrowed eyes,

'What is wrong with you today?'

She burned inside with humiliation at her lack of control. She was no better than the swooning legions of girls who gathered in the kitchens on each floor of this impressive London headquarters to eulogise over his mythical sexual prowess and inestimable wealth.

'Nothing,' Lucy muttered, and called on every bit of training she had to regain her composure. When she heard him shut his door behind them and follow her in she closed her eyes for a split second and took deep breaths. She chastised herself roundly. This job was so important; the sharp increase in wages meant that she was finally able to take care of her mother properly.

She couldn't jeopardise all that now by turning into a bumbling, stumbling, mooning idiot—no matter how gorgeous her boss happened to be. A voice mocked her inwardly. It wasn't as if she even *wanted* a man like him to notice her. She *had to* control these wayward thoughts. They disturbed her more than she cared to admit, making her think of long-buried memories of her childhood.

It should be easy enough to do after witnessing that last little scene. Evidently Aristotle Levakis went for quivering, highly strung thoroughbreds, all lean and sleek with good bloodlines. Lucy Proctor was more along the lines of a…a placid cart horse, and her bloodline was considerably less blue than he was used to. More of a murky brown.

She watched as Levakis came back around the other side of his desk and gestured impatiently for her to sit down and take notes, not even glancing her way. Lucy willed her heartbeat to slow down and sat, legs tucked under the chair demurely, pen poised over a blank sheet of paper, and prayed that her skirt wouldn't split open.

Aristotle Levakis stood behind his desk, hands deep in the pockets of his trousers, and looked at the demurely bent head of his new assistant. It was most irritating to be faced with the fact that Augustine Archer had forced him to reject her by demanding more of a commitment than he was prepared to give right now. To any woman.

His assistant shifted in her seat minutely, making Ari's eyes narrow on her. That ripple of awareness ran through him *again*. It was faint, elusive, yet irritatingly insistent, and had been ever since she'd walked into his office two months before in a primly structured suit.

An uncomfortable suspicion made him tense inwardly;

was it this *awareness* that had had an effect on the lessening and ultimate annihilation of his desire for Augustine Archer? Her shrieked words still vibrated in the air, but at that moment Aristotle would be hard pushed to bring her image to mind. Immediately as he realised the import of what he was thinking he rejected the notion as utterly absurd.

Lucy Proctor, his relatively new assistant, was as far removed from his habitual choice of lover as could be humanly possible. He couldn't believe he was even giving a second of his time to this subject, or putting those two words *Lucy* and *lover* in the same sentence, but almost against his will his eyes flicked down from shiny, albeit non-descript dark brown hair to where her knees were tight together, legs tucked under the chair.

His almost contemptuous regard stopped for a moment to take in what could only be described as wantonly voluptuous thighs encased far too snugly in the confines of a pencil skirt. Irritation prickled stronger. He would have to have a word with the head of Human Resources and tell her to pass on a discreet message about the code of dress he expected from his assistant. And yet his expert eye hadn't missed the surprisingly small waist, cinched in by a belt. That realisation stung him.

He tried to reassert his self-control. She was big…all over… His eyes flicked back up to the line of more than generous breasts under her silk shirt. And yet, prompted a little rogue voice, she looked as firm as a succulent peach. And her face…that was something he realised now he hadn't really given much time to study, seeing her only as someone employed to do his bidding, but now, much to his chagrin, his gaze wanted to stop and linger. Look properly. Take in the surprisingly graceful curve of a well-defined cheekbone. Aristotle's blood was starting to heat up; with a kind of desperation he noted that she wore glasses, as if that might have the effect of a cold douche on his suddenly raging hormones.

It didn't. He battled with his libido but it seemed determined to confound him, and he wondered what on earth was precipitating this reaction when Lucy had worked for his company for two years already. He'd only met her intermittently in that time, as she'd worked for his legal counsel, and she certainly hadn't had any discernible effect on him then. But now she was his assistant, and a welcome relief after dealing with a succession of simpering, moon-eyed idiots.

With that in mind, he called on all his powers of logic to explain the bizarre anomaly of his physical reaction, and finally felt some equanimity return: he was a red-blooded male, he was bound to respond arbitrarily to some women, even only passably attractive ones.

Except this wasn't the first time: he uncomfortably recalled one morning when he'd stepped into the staff elevator, because his own private one had been closed for repairs. Someone had run to stop the doors closing and launched themselves into the lift with such force that they'd careened into him. He'd felt every contour and curve of a very lush female body plastered against his for a second. It had been Lucy.

The memory seared him now. She'd been as curvaceous as something brought to life from a painting by Rubens, and the minute she'd walked into his office to interview for this job he'd remembered that moment in annoyingly vivid detail. Right now all he could think about was how she'd felt pressed against him. Especially when compared to the more sparingly built Augustine Archers of this world.

Lucy Proctor had shown no hint of remembering the moment in the lift, though, and Aristotle certainly wasn't going to admit to such a chink in his own legendary control. But when she sat in front of him now, the vision of her thighs straining against that too-tight skirt on the periphery of his vision, he could feel his body responding to her with a strength that disturbed him—a strength almost beyond his control…

The object of his uncharacteristic pondering looked up then quizzically, clearly wondering why he wasn't saying anything. Irrational rage rushed through him. He wasn't used to being rendered speechless like this. But in that moment, as if to compound every other revelation, he noticed she had the most unusually coloured eyes: a dark slaty grey that was almost blue, framed with the longest blackest lashes. Her mouth opened, as if to speak, and entirely against his will his eyes moved down. He'd not noticed until now that she had a sizeable gap between her front teeth. It was all at once innocent and unbelievably erotic.

Shocking and out of nowhere Aristotle had a sudden vision of those lips wrapped around a part of his anatomy, those almond-shaped eyes looking up into his as she— Lust exploded into his brain and turned everything red.

Lucy looked up at her boss and her mouth went dry. Her pulse, which had finally started slowing down, picked up pace again and she could feel herself grow hot. He was looking at her with such intensity that for a moment she thought— Instantly she shut down those rogue thoughts, and as if she'd imagined it the lines in his face tightened. He was positively glowering at her. Inwardly she quivered, outwardly she clung onto her poise and acknowledged that it was no wonder his adversaries hadn't ever got the better of him.

'Sir?' she said, thankful that her voice sounded cool and calm, unruffled.

He kept glowering at her for another long moment, and Lucy felt inexplicably as if some sort of battle of wills she was unaware of was going on.

Eventually he bit out, 'I think you can start calling me Aristotle.'

His voice sounded rough. She guessed it must be the remnants of his anger at the recent scene, but even so Lucy's belly quivered. She knew some close colleagues called him Aristotle, and she'd heard the beautiful blonde requesting breathily to speak to *'Ari'* when she'd phoned before the dramatics this morning, but the thought of addressing this man by his first name was having a seismic effect on her whole body.

'Very well,' she finally managed to get out. But couldn't bring herself to actually say it.

Aristotle sat down as if he hadn't just invited her to call him something far more intimate than *Sir*, or *Mr Levakis*, and proceeded to dictate with such lightning speed that it took all of Lucy's wits and concentration to keep up. In truth she was glad of the distraction, but by the time he was done her head was ringing.

He dismissed her with a brusque flick of his hand, his head already buried in some paperwork, and Lucy stood up. She was at the door when she heard a curt, 'Oh, and see to it, please, that Augustine Archer is sent something…'

Lucy turned around, and the look of dark cynicism she saw on Levakis' face made her draw in a breath.

'…*suitable*.'

Lucy looked at him, nonplussed for a moment. Her previous boss had never made such a request. Did he mean…?

As if he could read her mind, Aristotle said ascerbically, 'That's exactly what I mean. I don't care who you call, just make sure it's expensive, anything but a ring, and send it over with a note. I'll e-mail you the address.'

Lucy's hand was clutching the door, and she didn't know why this feeling of something like disappointment was curling through her. Anyone with half a brain cell would have been able to tell her this was exactly how a man like him operated. And wasn't it confirmation of another rumour about him?

How well he compensated his lovers? But still…he wasn't even taking the time to compose a note himself.

She forced herself to sound non-committal. 'How would you like the note to read?'

He shrugged one broad shoulder and smiled sardonically, cruelly. 'Make it up. What kind of platitude would *you* like to hear from a man who has just dumped you?' His mouth twisted even more. 'I think it's safe to say that someone like Ms Archer will throw away the card and move straight to the main prize, so I wouldn't worry about it too much. Just keep it as impersonal as possible.'

Shock at his cold words impacted Lucy right in her belly. Her face must have given something away, because Aristotle lounged back in his chair and looked at her with a dangerous gleam in those fascinating green eyes.

'You don't approve of my methods?'

Lucy could feel a tide of heat climb up from her chest. She alternately shook and nodded her head, and some garbled words came out. 'Not at all…' She realised what she'd said and groaned inwardly when she saw a flash of something dark cross his face. She could not let her own personal opinion of his behaviour jeopardise this job. Too much now depended on her wages.

She gestured clumsily. 'I mean, I have no problem doing as you suggest. Your methods…are your methods. It's not for me to judge.'

He sat up and raised a brow, and Lucy wondered dismally how on earth they had got onto this. She wanted to be back outside, with a wall and door between them, catching her breath and restoring her equilibrium, not discussing how best to let his mistress down.

But he said, 'So you admit there is something to judge, then?'

Lucy shook her head, drowning in heat now. 'No—look,

I'm sorry, I'm not being very articulate. I'll do as you ask and make sure that the accompanying note is appropriate.' She added hurriedly, 'I can show it to you before I send it…?'

He shook his head and his face became impassive, hard. Lucy stood there for another moment, not sure what to do and then he bit out,

'That'll be all.'

Stung, and more than mortified, Lucy mumbled something incoherent and fled, shutting the door behind her. Amidst the embarrassment, anger surged—why was she surprised or, worse, disappointed? She'd seen this kind of behaviour from men all her life.

But still, what an *absolute*— She halted her racing thoughts as she sat behind her desk and fought to steady her breathing and hammering heart. The last five minutes was the closest she'd come to a personal discussion with her new boss. She should have just bowed her head and walked out. She cursed her expressive face. Her mother had always told her it would get her into trouble. And hadn't it just? Her inherent distaste for his coldly generous dismissive treatment of his ex-mistress hadn't been well hidden enough. But the truth was it had tapped into a deeply buried pain, a very familiar pain. She'd witnessed the other side of someone on the receiving end of that treatment. Over and over again.

Lucy shuddered inwardly when she woke her computer from sleep and struggled to concentrate on work. Aristotle's cynical view of how Ms Archer would receive his gift was no doubt spot-on; hadn't she witnessed her own mother reduced to that level after years of similar treatment? Although Augustine Archer didn't strike her as the kind of woman who had to survive on hand-outs. No, this was a different league. Lucy's soft mouth tightened as bile rose from her belly. That kind of so-called *main prize* would have been just the kind of thing her mother would have used to pay for Lucy's school uniform for another year—the sort of thing that had financed their lives.

Lucy forced her anger down. She had to think of her boss purely in professional terms. What he did or how he acted personally was none of her business. She didn't have to like him; she just had to work for him.

Thank goodness she'd forged a different path. She would never be beholden to any man or, worse, held in his sexual or financial thrall. She'd worked too hard and her mother had sacrificed too much to make sure she avoided exactly that scenario. Just as her computer screen came back to life and she saw her bespectacled face momentarily reflected on the dark surface she felt unmitigated relief that she need never fear the kind of attention her mother and women like Augustine Archer courted. She was safe from all of that.

Aristotle watched the closed door for an inordinate amount of time. Heat still coursed through his body—heat that confounded him and every effort he made to try and dampen it. All he could see in his mind's eye was the sway of that well-rounded bottom as she'd stopped by the door, and how he'd blurted out the first thing that had come into his head, as if he'd had to stop her, not let her leave.

He flung himself back in his seat and raked a hand through unruly hair, unusually diverted from work. He cursed the fact again that he'd had to let Augustine go at this point in negotiations. He briefly considered wooing her back, but his fists clenched in rejection of that idea. He would never debase himself by grovelling to a woman—not for *anything*.

He considered the request he'd just made of Lucy; he'd always made the call to a jewellers himself before, and would instruct them to compose a suitably impersonal note. Usually it wasn't even a note—just his name. A clear indication that whatever he and the particular woman had shared was over and she shouldn't come calling again. And invariably they knew not to. Few were as impertinent as Augustine Archer, confronting him directly. His mouth twisted in recognition of the fact that as he got older and remained single he represented some kind of irresistible challenge to those women.

He diverted his thoughts from an area he didn't want to investigate: that of having to contemplate giving up his freedom, which he knew would be inevitable at some stage. The future was unavoidable. He would have to find a suitable wife and produce an heir, purely to protect all that he was now putting in place from the greedy clutches of others.

The prospect evoked no more emotion in him than mild uninterest and irritation. He'd long ago learnt the lesson of what marriage really meant—at the age of five, when his father had introduced Helen Savakis as his new stepmother and she'd quickly shown him the cold hatred she had for a son who wasn't her own. Whatever dim and distant memories Ari might have had of his mother, who'd died when he was four, and a halcyon time that might never have existed except in some childish fanciful memory bank, had long been quashed and buried.

The fact that those nebulous memories rose to haunt him in dreams so vivid that he sometimes woke in tears was a shameful weakness he'd always been determined to ignore. It was one reason he'd never spent a full night with a woman.

As if drawn by a magnet his thoughts again went to his assistant, who was fast assuming a place in his imagination that he did not welcome. Why had he felt goaded into saying all he just had? And then been surprised by the blatant look of distaste on her face—annoyed by it? And he had not left it at that but engaged her in a dialogue about it. As if he even cared what her opinion of him was! He was aware of a niggling desire that he'd wanted to see her somehow...rattled. Since she'd been working for him she'd always seemed to fade into the background, barely noticeable.

But he *was* noticing her and she *had* just reacted, her cheeks flushing prettily. He frowned at that. Since when had he started thinking of her as pretty? And since when had he been interested in *pretty*?

And, not only that, what on earth had compelled him to tell her to call him Aristotle when he'd always preferred his PAs to call him Mr Levakis? It was something in the way she'd looked up at him and said *sir*.

In a bid to restore some order to his life, which seemed to be morphing out of all recognition, he rang through to Lucy and gave her the name and number of the latest English socialite who had been chasing him, instructing her to set up a date for that evening. He ignored the way even her voice seemed to send a frisson of reaction straight to his groin. With that done he felt some semblance of calm wash over him. Life would return to normal. He would forget all about this bizarre obsession with his secretary's far too provocatively well-built body and concentrate on the merger.

The following morning, when Lucy was walking the short distance from her bus stop to work, she still burned with mortification. In her hand she carried a small overnight bag which held a change of clothes and some evening wear. She'd taken a call from the head of Human Resources the day before and been informed stoutly that she needed to think a little more thoroughly about the way she dressed, and that it might be a good idea to have a change of clothes in the office at all times to cover for emergencies. Like too-tight skirts, she thought churlishly. The fact that Levakis had gone over her head and asked someone to speak to her made her skin crawl with humiliation—not to mention the fact that he'd obviously noticed her bursting out of that skirt.

With getting her mother settled in her new home she simply
hadn't had time since she'd started working for him to kit
herself out with a new wardrobe, despite being given a
generous allowance to do so. It had been full-on from day one.

Luckily last night had been late-night shopping, and
Levakis had left relatively early for the date Lucy had set up
for him. Her belly clenched at the thought of that. The woman
she'd rung hadn't been in the slightest bit fazed that Aristotle
himself hadn't bothered to call, and of course she'd been free
at a moment's notice. A wave of disgust washed through Lucy
and she pushed it down along with bitter memories. She didn't
care what he did or who he did it with. A voice mocked her
inwardly: who was *she* to judge anyway?

Just at that moment the heavens opened from a slate-grey
sky and Lucy yelped as torrential rain poured down, comprehensively drenching her in seconds. *No*! She ran across the
road towards the refuge of the huge gleaming Levakis
building, her mind filled with the fact that they had an important meeting to attend in less than an hour on the other side
of London.

Aristotle strode through the reception area, raking a hand
through rain-wet hair, and mentally cursed the inclement
English weather which had momentarily darkened the
enormous glass atrium. He stepped into his own private lift—
no possibility of a lush, curvaceous body colliding with his
today—and stabbed at the button to whisk him all the way to
the top of the building, irritated beyond belief to be thinking
of that *again*. Was he actually hoping for it? he asked himself
derisively.

His starkly handsome face was reflected back to him in the
steel surface of the door, but he didn't see that as the lift
zoomed skyward. No, what he saw and what he relived was
the fact that last night he'd taken a beautiful *available* woman

on a date and she had done nothing for him. His mouth
twisted. It hadn't been for lack of trying on her part, or even
on his, which had been a novel sensation.

In a bid not to be dictated to by his malfunctioning
hormones, he'd escorted Arabella—*or had it been Mirabella*?—up to her apartment, but had realised with sickening
inevitability that nothing would be happening. With her,
anyway. He'd been rendered impotent from the waist down.
She'd become petulant and increasingly desperate, seeing
correctly that she hadn't managed to snare Aristotle's interest,
and he'd had to extricate himself with more diplomacy than
a head of state during peace negotiations.

So now, as he strode out of his lift and towards his main
office, he was thoroughly disgruntled. Ignoring the assistants
sitting meekly at their desks in the ante-room that preceded
his and Lucy's offices, he opened the door and took a breath,
preparing to fire a series of commands at the woman who had
been the singular cause of his unsatisfying night.

But the office was empty.

He had the most curious sensation of his belly hollowing
out before he heard movement coming from the door which
led into the bathroom just off their offices. While he had a
private bathroom too, this more communal bathroom had a
shower and a dressing room, which Aristotle availed himself
of whenever he was required to go straight to a function from
work.

Closing the main door quietly behind him, without really
being aware of what he was doing, he walked silently into the
office. He heard a muffled curse and then something drop.

Feeling like a voyeur, and not liking it, he halted by the
door which lay slightly ajar. Through the crack he saw Lucy,
and when his eyes registered what he was seeing his whole
body locked, every muscle taut. Unable to move, all he could
do was take in the sight with widening eyes. Lucy's wet hair

hung in long dark tendrils over luminously pale shoulders. She was bending over to pull trousers up over long, surprisingly slender legs. Her legs led upwards to those shapely thighs, which curved out to a lushly rounded bottom encased in some kind of black lace and silk concoction.

She wriggled her bottom and her hips as she pulled the trousers up fully, and then twisted towards Aristotle to tie the fastening at the side. Heat engulfed him. His blood hummed and his heart picked up an unsteady beat. Facing him as she did, both hands to one side, her perfectly formed breasts were enticingly pushed together and towards him with unknowing and unbelievably erotic appeal. Her bra looked hardly adequate to contain the generous mounds of alabaster flesh— he wondered dimly if any of her clothes fitted properly. And who would have known that she'd have such exotic tastes in undergarments underneath that prim exterior? Arousal soared.

Another muffled curse came as an even longer tendril of dark hair swung over her shoulder and clung wetly to the slope of one unashamedly voluptuous breast. Aristotle's gaze moved up with supreme difficulty, and he saw that gap in her front teeth as she bit her lip, a hectic flush across her cheeks.

As if entranced by a siren song, he couldn't move. His gaze slid down again and took in that small waist, which he'd only noted yesterday, and her belly, which was sucked in to help with the obstinate fastening. It was soft but gently contoured, as if she fought some kind of battle to keep her body in check but it was determined to thwart her efforts and retain its inherently seductive softness. Her hips flared out generously from that waist with such hourglass perfection Aristotle felt momentarily dizzy.

Abruptly she moved, having at last managed to fasten her trousers, and straightened. Her belly was still sucked in, pushing her breasts out even more as she reached for something else which Aristotle could see was a shirt.

His brain wouldn't function. He couldn't move. All he could see was Lucy and her half-naked body, that long dark hair clinging provocatively to her skin like wet skeins of silk.

That thing that he called *awareness* had just exploded into full-on lust.

Lucy yanked the tag off her new shirt and pulled it on impatiently, all fingers and thumbs on the buttons of the slippery grey silk material. She'd never have gone for something like this normally, but after being hauled over the coals the day before she'd known that she had no choice but to buy the kind of uniform that someone like Aristotle Levakis would expect—and that meant expense, and things like silk as opposed to cotton. She breathed out thankfully. At least she'd had that change of clothes. No way could she have faced him this morning looking like the drowned rat she'd been just moments before.

With the shirt finally closed she tucked it in hurriedly and desperately listened out for a heavy footfall or the door opening. She knew he was due in any minute—he was more punctual than any boss she'd ever known. That had to be the reason her heart was thumping so hard: the fear of being caught like this. She raked a brush through her hair, wincing as it caught on the still-damp strands, and quickly twisted it up into a chignon of sorts. It would have to do.

Slipping her feet into flat shoes, she stuck her glasses back on, gathered up her wet things, looked up—and stopped breathing. In the crack of the open door her boss was just standing there, looking at her.

CHAPTER TWO

How long had he been standing there? The words barely impinged on Lucy's consciousness. She was too full of raging heat, embarrassment, and something more disturbing.

On some self-protective level she refused to believe he had seen her yanking her clothes on with all the grace of a baby elephant. He wasn't moving. He looked slightly shell-shocked, and mortification rushed through Lucy. She managed to move and opened the door fully, gabbling something she hoped was coherent to fill the awful silence.

'I got caught in the rain shower. I was just changing.'

She stepped out and past Aristotle, who turned to follow her with his eyes as she retreated to the safe zone behind her desk, not even sure why she needed to feel safe.

When she could bring herself to look at him, she registered that his hair was damp, his suit slightly wet. She met his eyes, and in that instant something passed between them, something electric and elemental, and Lucy knew that he *had* seen her dressing—even though stubbornly she still refused to believe it. She recoiled from the uncomfortable awareness deep within her. It scared the life out of her.

Still babbling, she said, 'Looks like you got caught too. Do you want to change before we go? I've instructed Julian to have the car downstairs in fifteen minutes, and I can have your suit sent out to be cleaned.'

Aristotle, seemingly completely unconcerned about the meeting or changing his clothes, lounged back against the doorjamb and crossed his arms. His gaze swept down over Lucy's outfit and she cringed, wondering if she'd left a tag on somewhere. She fought the urge to check herself.

He just continued to look at her with that disturbing intensity before saying, 'Tell me, did you wear that skirt yesterday on purpose? Aware of how provocative it was?'

Shock, disbelief and cold horror slammed into Lucy. Her mouth opened for a moment but nothing emerged. She couldn't articulate, but finally managed a strangled, 'Of *course* not. I would never be so…' Words failed her again and she closed her mouth helplessly.

Aristotle could see injured pride straighten her spine, the shock on her face. He had the absurd impulse to apologise, but couldn't help remembering the way she'd looked so wantonly luscious in it, straining against the material. He could imagine inching it up over those pale quivering thighs as she stood with her back against him, how the full globes of her bottom would press into him as he pushed her forward over his desk, reaching down between them to hitch her skirt higher and free his own— *What the hell was wrong with him?* His mind never deviated to lurid sexual fantasies with so little provocation.

He stood away from the door abruptly and curtly informed Lucy to make sure she had all the necessary papers and documents required for the meeting ready. He then went into the dressing room and breathed deep, as if he could inhale some common sense. But instead an evocatively feminine scent teased his nostrils and brought the last few minutes vividly back. Along with his libido.

With a growl of intense irritation Aristotle yanked a clean

suit from the well-stocked wardrobe and stripped off to step into the shower, turning it onto cold. It did little to help.

Lucy flinched minutely and scowled at her computer when she heard the phone being slammed down in her boss's office. He'd just taken a call from his half-brother in Athens, and while he never seemed to welcome those calls he usually acted with more restraint than that. She shook her head. He'd been in a foul humour for two weeks now. *Ever since that morning.* Heat still crawled over her skin when she thought of the way he'd lounged against the door and looked at her, and mentioned that skirt. *He believed she might have worn it like that on purpose.*

And yet since then he had proceeded to treat her either as if a) he couldn't bring himself even to mention her name, or b) as if he might turn to stone if he so much as looked at her for longer than two seconds.

Lucy had to assure herself that nothing *had* happened, and if anything this was just a normal working relationship. Aristotle was famous for his brusque, no-nonsense approach. What had she expected? Warm and fuzzy? She shifted in her seat uncomfortably, the fact was she did feel inordinately *warm*—especially when he was around. She also felt constantly on edge, as if a kind of prickly heat lay just under the surface of her skin. She felt achy and jittery, but no symptoms of a flu or a cold had developed, so she couldn't put it down to that. She was beginning to despair of ever having any sense of equilibrium again. At times like this she longed for the uncomplicated working relationship she'd had with her last boss. Her mouth quirked wryly. But then, he had been nearing seventy, well past retirement age, and had a huge typically Greek family.

Lucy nearly shot out of her chair when she heard a coolly drawled, 'Something funny on the internet today?'

She quickly pressed a key so that her blank document disappeared, and took a breath before looking up, steeling herself. She had to steel herself a lot around this man. She smiled brightly, but it faded when she saw something dark cross his face.

'No… I was just…going over the latest mail from the Parnassus Corporation.'

She mentally crossed her fingers and breathed a sigh of relief, because that was exactly what she *had* been doing—*before* she'd been looking at a blank document for minutes on end like some moon-eyed idiot.

Aristotle emerged from his office and prowled towards Lucy. Her blood-rate shot up.

'Liar,' he said softly.

Her back straightened. 'Excuse me?'

He came to her desk and rested on his hands over it, looming over her. She fought against shrinking back as his eyes bored into hers. It was making her dizzy after days of only the most cursory eye contact.

He arched one slashing dark brow. 'If that's the case, tell me what Parnassus proposes we do in the final stages of sealing the merger?'

Lucy looked up, spellbound. As if from a long way away her more rational and professional self, the one that wasn't melting into a puddle in her chair, came back. Miraculously, information came into her brain, and she clung onto it like a life-raft.

Unable to break eye contact, and feeling as if her voice had been dipped in rust, Lucy said, 'He…he suggests that the final stages take place in Athens, as that's where the two companies originated one hundred years ago. He thinks it should be there that the merger is finally revealed. He wants it to be a triumphant homecoming to the country he and his family fled from when he was young, and for Athens to be the symbolic and actual birthplace of the greatest merger in Greek shipping and industrial history.'

Silence lengthened and tautened between them. Electric awareness quivered in the air until finally Aristotle just said quietly, 'Good. And I presume you have everything in order for you to travel to Athens for three weeks?'

Lucy just blinked stupidly for a moment as numerous things impacted her brain. Primarily the fact that she hadn't actually considered the fact that *of course* she'd be expected to go to Athens too, in little over a week from now.

All she could say was, 'Yes, I do,' when in actual fact for some reason—even though it had been talked about for weeks—she'd never considered for a moment that she'd be accompanying Aristotle on such a prestigious engagement.

Her lack of foresight mocked her; of course it had to be her, no one else had had access to all the vital and top secret information—information so secret that she'd had to sign a contract the day she'd been hired, forbidding her to divulge any information to anyone. If she committed such an offence it could see her being fired on the spot, and certainly ruined for any future employment within these circles...

The full enormity of the size of this merger and the importance of the man in front of her started to sink in very belatedly. Mortifyingly, Lucy knew that a large part of her distraction had to do with finding herself working for someone who had reached into a secret part of her and shaken her up so much that she had to spend an inordinate amount of time just denying it to herself. Even now, as he still loomed over her, she denied it to herself.

She reassured herself desperately that she was just reacting to Aristotle Levakis' undeniable charisma, like any other red-blooded human being.

With that in mind she took a sheaf of papers that needed filing off her desk and stood up, clutching them to her chest.

It was a blatant attempt to put some distance between them. Aristotle straightened too, and with arms folded surveyed her closely. That treacherous heat pooled within her again, but now she knew what it was she could deflect her own reaction to it.

She hitched up her chin. 'Was there anything else?'

He shook his head slowly and a lazy smile curved his lips. Lucy felt like clinging onto something.

'No, that's all for now.' He turned to go back to his office, but just when Lucy was about to let out a sigh of relief he turned back. With his forearm resting high on the doorjamb, drawing her eye to his long and hard muscled body, he said, 'Don't forget we have that engagement tonight. Be ready to leave at six-thirty. I'll get dressed in my office; you can use the dressing room.'

He disappeared into his own office then, shutting the door behind him, and Lucy all but sagged onto the floor in a heap. She *had* forgotten all about the function they were to attend that night. She cursed herself as she sank down heavily into her chair. What was wrong with her? Forgetting the function, not realising she would have to go to Athens… Her brain was turning to mush. And in this job that was not a luxury she could afford.

How could she have forgotten that terse conversation just days ago, when he'd said to her with a grimace on his face, 'You're going to have to come to the Black and White Ball with me.'

Lucy's belly had clenched. She'd expected that she might have to accompany her boss to some functions, but with Aristotle's extremely healthy social life she hadn't considered it would become a reality so soon. And did he have to look so reluctant at the prospect?

She'd ignored the ridiculous feeling of hurt and asked hopefully, 'But surely there must be someone else…' *anyone else* '…you could call?'

After all, as she'd restrained herself from pointing out, last-minute dates were not something he shied away from. He'd had more than a few since the Honourable Augustine Archer and then the even more Honourable Mirabella Ashton, each one well-documented in the press that gloried in his playboy exploits. And yet the morning after each date he'd appeared taciturn and as irritable as she'd ever seen him.

He'd curtly instructed her to send each night's delectation a disgustingly expensive bunch of flowers. Lucy had cynically assumed that none of the women were performing well enough to hold his interest and merit a piece of jewellery.

It was then that she'd realised that she hadn't arranged a date for him in at least a week. The thought had unsettled her more than she'd liked to admit.

He'd looked at her with narrowed eyes. 'As I am currently partnerless, not that it's any of your business, I've decided that *you* will accompany me. Do you have a problem with that?'

Feeling sick, Lucy had shaken her head rapidly. She had to stop reacting to this man and provoking him. 'No. Not at all. I'll put it in the diary now.'

Lucy came back to the present moment. She was still holding the sheaf of papers clutched to her chest like some kind of shield. She looked at the open diary beside her and there in stark letters was written *'Black and White Ball, Park Lane Hotel. Seven p.m.'* The thought of spending any more time than was absolutely necessary with this man was causing nothing short of sheer panic inside her.

She put down the papers and picked up the phone to make a call to the home where her mother was resident. She asked them to pass on the message that she wouldn't be able to visit that evening.

The matron on the other end said gently, 'I'll pass on the message, Lucy love, but you do know that it won't make any difference, don't you?'

Lucy felt very alone all of a sudden. She swallowed back the ever-present guilt, pain and grief, and nodded even though the other woman couldn't see her. Her voice was thick with emotion. 'I know…but I'd appreciate it all the same, if you don't mind.'

Lucy could hear Aristotle moving around in his own office as she changed in the dressing room. This was a formal event, so she had to wear a long dress, and the one she looked at now in the mirror was perfectly respectable—if completely boring. It was black, which meant it was slimming, and it had a high neck which covered her breasts adequately. Anything that did that was fine with her. And anyway, she told herself stoutly, she wasn't dressing to impress, she was dressing to accompany her boss in a work capacity.

She left her hair up and put on some make-up: mascara and a little blusher. Then, slipping her feet into a pair of plain black high heels, she picked up her weekend bag stuffed with her work clothes and took a deep breath before walking out, feeling ridiculously nervous and hating herself for it.

That breath hitched in her throat and her brain stopped functioning when she saw Aristotle emerge from his own office, resplendent in a traditional tuxedo. The black made him look even darker, and very dangerous. Lucy fought back the wave of awareness, her hands gripping her bag.

He looked up from adjusting his cufflinks then, and the snowy perfection of his shirt made the green of his eyes pop out. He ran quick eyes over Lucy, making her squirm inwardly before quirking a brow and saying mockingly, 'Well, if you're trying to fade into the background it's already working.'

Lucy swallowed past a dry throat. 'I'm your assistant, not your date.'

More's the pity, Aristotle surprised himself with thinking as he took her in, just a few feet away. Although not in that dress. It was basically a sack: a black sack covering her from neck to toe. It might as well have been a burkha for all he could see of her body, and he knew with a hunger that had been growing day by day and minute by minute that he very much wanted to see her body showcased in something much more revealing and *tight*. Like that skirt which had assumed mythic proportions in his fantasies. He beat back an intense surge of desire, in spite of the awful dress, and noted the hectic flush on her cheeks, the wary glitter of her eyes.

She was intriguing him more and more—not only with her luscious curves, but in the way she reacted to him, his spikily quick responses. Every expression was an open book as it crossed her face. She wasn't afraid of him, and that was heady in itself. That she didn't approve of him was glaringly obvious, and it was a novel sensation to have that from a woman.

Aristotle was looking at her far too assessingly. Lucy's belly quivered in response and she told herself sternly that she *wasn't* responding to him; she was just responding to the charisma of the man.

But then he strolled towards her nonchalantly and she had to fight the urge to turn tail and run. He walked around her as if inspecting a horse, and she turned around, unable to bear the thought of him looking at her too-large bottom. She cursed her genes again and felt acutely self-conscious. Why couldn't she be a slim, petite little thing like her mother?

Her voice was high and defensive. 'Is there something wrong? This dress fits perfectly well. It's not too tight, if that's what you're afraid of.' She wouldn't be making *that* mistake again.

Aristotle's eyes flicked to hers. They glittered with something dark and indefinable.

'The dress is fine. For an old lady.'

Lucy sucked in a shocked breath. She'd spent a small

fortune from her allowance on this dress. But before she could say anything he was gesturing to her head.

'It's too late to do anything about the dress, but leave down your hair. You look like you're going to work.'

His normally accentless voice had lapsed into something unmistakably Greek, and it resonated within Lucy. Her mind blanked and her hand went up instinctively in a protective gesture. Her hair was part of her armour, she suddenly realised. No way could she take it down. She might as well just strip off the dress and stand in front of him in her under-wear. Treacherous heat licked through her again, making a mockery of her attempts to rationalise it. She shook her head dumbly.

His eyes held hers and he just said quietly, 'Take it down Lucy.' It was so utterly shocking to be standing in front of her boss and have him speak to her like this, that Lucy found herself obeying him. With extreme reluctance she took out the pins from the back. She could feel her hair loosen and fall with annoying and heavily layered predictability around her shoulders and down her back.

Aristotle fisted his hands in his trouser pockets to stop them reaching out to feel the texture of that heavy silky mass of hair. It was darker than he'd originally thought, and luxu-riously unruly, reaching down as far as her shoulderblades. He had an image of her reclining back on a sumptuous divan, tendrils of that glorious hair over her shoulders and trailing over her the tops of her bare— *Get a grip, man*! With a supreme effort of will Aristotle reined himself in and said gut-turally, 'That's better. *Now* you look as if you're ready for a function. Let's go.'

With an easy and automatic courtesy which surprised Lucy, and she wasn't sure why that was, he took her case from her white-knuckle grip and led the way out of the office. She stumbled as she followed his graceful stride down the corridor to his private lift. She had a moment of dithering, stupidly wondering if she should take the staff lift just a few feet further down, but as if reading her mind *again* Aristotle flicked her an impatient glance and she stepped in.

It was only when they were ensconced in the lift that the memory of the last time she'd shared such a space with him came back in all its glory.

She couldn't help her reaction flowering. Too much had happened since then. Now she stood there, with her hair down, feeling as exposed as if he'd just run his hands over her naked flesh—especially when she recalled his look from moments ago, a look that had to have been some projection of her own awful, twisted feelings. The tall man beside her oozed with sexual heat. She could smell him and feel him. Suddenly she had the strangest sensation of holding something huge back… Wanton images hovered tantalisingly on the periphery of her mind and threatened to burst through, mocking her for a control that was beginning to feel very shaky.

Lucy gritted her jaw and looked resolutely up at the display as the lift seemed to inch downwards, willing it with every fibre of her being to go faster.

The effort it took to stay apart from Lucy in that lift, amidst a rush of memories of how she had felt pressed against him, which once again stunned him with their vividness, washed away Aristotle's last resistance where this woman was concerned. He'd never experienced this level of sexual awareness before, and in truth frustration was a novel sensation when he was so used to getting what he wanted, when he wanted. He didn't stop to question his decision or his motives for a second.

It was quite simple. He had to have this woman in his bed—and as a soon as possible. He would sleep with her. Then she would lose her allure and this bizarre spell she held over him would be broken. In three months he could let her go. Or less, if he got bored. According to her contract he could terminate employment with due notice; she, however, could not walk away unless she wanted to seriously sabotage her career. Because of the top secret nature of the merger she was tied to Levakis Enterprises until the whole thing became public.

Work, which he'd always strictly compartmentalised as separate from pleasure, would become pleasure—*his* pleasure. And Lucy's too. He wanted her with him every inch of the way as he took her again and again to sate this burning ache. Somehow instinctively he knew that one night would not be enough, and it made him uncomfortable to acknowledge it.

Nevertheless, as the lift descended the final few floors, a fizz of anticipation ran through Aristotle's veins and he felt truly alive for the first time in a long time. Even thoughts of the merger were receding into a background place. A dim and distant alarm bell sounded at the back of his mind, but he was too fired up to notice or dwell on it.

The lift juddered softly to a stop and the doors swished open. He stood back and gestured for Lucy to precede him, looking at her carefully as she did so. She was avoiding his eye with all the finesse of a guilty-looking six-year-old caught with her hand in the cookie jar.

She stumbled slightly stepping out of the lift, and Aristotle took her bare silky smooth arm just above the elbow. The frisson of pleasure that went through him nearly made him sway. He could feel the swell of her breast tease his fingers and a primal instinct to possess this woman coursed through him. The fact that she held herself so rigidly at his side didn't put him off. She was as unmistakably his as—for now—he was hers.

A colleague of Aristotle's had just walked away. Lucy watched him go with a feeling of mounting terror. She did not want to be alone with her boss.

They were standing side by side under the seductively soft lighting of the main ballroom in the exclusive London hotel when she heard his drawling query, 'You don't need your glasses? Or are you wearing contacts?'

She nearly choked on her sparkling water and lowered the drink carefully, realising without even making a reflex gesture to check that she had indeed forgotten her glasses. She could picture them right now, sitting on the vanity cabinet in the dressing room of the office. She flushed guiltily and sent a quick, fleeting look to Aristotle. Standing here in this milieu, with his tall, hard body just inches away, was making her nervous. It made her so nervous, in fact, that she didn't stop the truth from spilling out.

'They aren't prescription glasses.'

She saw him frown from the corner of her eyes. 'So why do you wear them?'

He sounded aghast, and Lucy had no doubt that he could not understand why any woman would knowingly want to make herself any less attractive than she already was. A sense of extreme vulnerability washed through her.

She shrugged minutely and avoided his eye. 'I started wearing them when I was looking for work after college.' She squirmed inwardly. How could she explain to this man that she'd grown sick and tired of prospective bosses ogling her sizeable assets rather than her CV? A memory made her shiver with distaste: her first boss, whispering lasciviously on more than one occasion that he liked *big girls*.

Ever since then Lucy had made sure to be covered up at all times, hair pulled back and glasses firmly on. Yet, uncomfortably, she had to acknowledge that she'd found working with Aristotle Levakis something of a relief in that she knew there was no way on this earth a man like him would look twice at her. That assertion suddenly seemed shaky.

As if to compound the feeling, from the corner of her eye

she could see Aristotle turn subtly, so that he had his back to the room full of people. She even saw one person in the act of approaching falter and turn away, as if he'd sent off some silent signal she couldn't see. She couldn't resist sending him another quick look. He had an expression on his face that caught and held her, and she couldn't look away.

His eyes flicked down to her breasts—in exactly the way she'd seen men do all her life, ever since she'd developed out of all proportion in her early teens. But instead of her usual feeling of disgust and invasion, to her shame and horror she could feel herself respond. Her breasts grew heavy, their tips tight and hard. For a cataclysmic moment she actually felt the novel desire to know what it would feel like to have this man touch them. Shock at the sheer physicality of her reaction made her feel clammy.

Aristotle's eyes glittered. A whisper of a smile hovered around his mouth and then he said, 'And did it work?'

Shame and chagrin rushed through Lucy. Was she really so weak? With one look this man was felling all her careful defences like a bowling ball sending skittles flying.

Her voice sounded strangled. 'I found that, yes, it did work.'

Until now.

Lucy felt like a trapped insect, flat on its back and helpless in the face of a looming predator. Determined to negate her disturbing reaction, she looked away and said crisply, 'Plenty of people wear glasses for cosmetic reasons. I would have thought that you'd approve.'

His voice was curt. 'Your CV and your work ethic speak for themselves, Lucy. You don't need to bolster your image by making it more businesslike.'

Too-tight skirts, yes. Glasses, no. Aristotle swallowed a growl of irritation at his wayward mind.

Lucy looked back. She was more than surprised at his easy

commendation of her ability. So far it was only the fact that she hadn't been let go that had given her any indication of how well she was doing her job. She had to fight the urge to cross her hands defensively over her chest, but that was ridiculous. He wouldn't be looking at her like that. He'd just been making a point.

She inclined her head and said, 'Fine. I won't wear them.' She bit back the reflex to say *sir*. The last thing she needed now was for him to repeat his request to call him Aristotle. What she did need was for this evening to be over as soon as possible and to have a whole two days away from this man, to get her head together and clear again. Especially when the prospect of spending three weeks in Athens with him loomed on the horizon like a threatening stormcloud.

A few hours later Lucy breathed a sigh of relief when the car drew to a smooth halt outside her apartment block in south London. She'd tried to insist on taking a cab from the hotel, but Aristotle wouldn't listen. Then she'd tried to insist that he be dropped home first, but again he'd been adamant.

She reached for the door on her side and looked back to say a crisp goodnight. Her ability to speak left her. Aristotle was lounging in the far corner like a huge, dark avenging angel. A surge of panic gripped her and she felt blindly for the door handle, all but scrambling in her haste to get out and away. But just as she opened the door, extending one leg out of the car, the awful sound of ripping material made her heart stop. An ominously cold breeze whistled across the tops of her thighs.

She looked down and her jaw dropped when she saw a huge rip extending down the side of her dress from mid-thigh to hem. Only peripherally was she aware that it must have snagged on something. Her white thighs gleamed up at her in the gloom.

As all this was impacting on her brain, she heard a coolly sardonic, 'You don't seem to have much luck with clothes, do you?'

The sensation of wanting the ground to open up and swallow her whole had never seemed more strong than at that moment. She heard Aristotle say something unintelligible to his driver and then he got out. Lucy couldn't move. She was terrified that if she did something else would rip and her entire dress might fall off. But then Aristotle was standing there, looking down at her with a mocking smile and extending a hand.

With the utmost reluctance she put her hand in his and felt the world tilt crazily as he pulled her up. With her other hand she scrabbled to hold her dress together. Her face felt as red as a traffic light. Aristotle now had a light grip on her arm, and Lucy noticed that he held her bag in his other hand.

That, and the way he was looking at her now, made her feel extremely threatened. *It was the way he'd been looking at her that morning in the office.*

She felt jittery and stiff all at once, and tried to get her arm back.

'It must have caught on something. I'll be fine from here. You must be impatient to get home.'

But Aristotle ignored her and easily steered them towards the path, not letting go for a second. Lucy's blood was starting to fizzle and hum in her veins. She tried again while keeping a desperate clasp on her ruined dress. 'Really, Mr Levakis, my door is just here.'

She even dug her heels in, but he called back to the driver, 'That's all, Julian. You can go. I'll get a cab from here.'

'You're sure, sir?' The driver's surprise was evident in his voice.

'Yes. Goodnight, Julian.'

And with that, before Lucy could formulate a word or acknowledge the escalation of pure mind-numbing panic in her breast, she was being led to her door and Aristotle was looking down at her with his trademark impatience.

'Your keys?'

Lucy spluttered. The driver was pulling away from the kerb, making her even more panicked. 'Mr Levakis, *really*, you don't have to do this. Please. Thank you for the lift, but you shouldn't have let Julian go. You'll never get a cab from here…'

He looked down at her, those green eyes utterly mesmerising. 'I thought I told you to call me Aristotle. Now, your keys? Please.'

Much like earlier, when he'd told her to take down her hair, Lucy found herself obeying. She knew on some dim, rational level that it was just shock. She awkwardly dug her keys out of her handbag, while trying not to let the dress gape open, and watched wordlessly when Aristotle took them and opened the door, leading them into the foyer and to the lift. He looked at her again with a quirked brow and Lucy said faintly, 'Sixth floor.'

As the lift lurched skyward Lucy felt somehow as though she must be dreaming. She'd wake any moment and it would be Monday morning and everything would be back to normal. But then the lift bell pinged loudly and Aristotle, *her boss*, was looking at her again expectantly. She had no choice but to step out and walk to her door a few feet away.

Her brain was refusing to function coherently. She simply could not start to pose the question, even to herself, as to what he was doing here. She turned at her door with a very strong need to make sure she went through it alone and this man stayed outside.

She held out her hand for her keys, which he still held. She couldn't look him in the eye. The bright fluorescence of the lighting was too unforgiving and harsh. Although she knew that it wouldn't dent his appeal.

'Thank you for seeing me safely in.'

'You're not in yet.'

With more panic than genuine irritation Lucy sent him a fulminating glance and grabbed her keys. She opened the door with a hand that was none too steady. She could have wept with relief when the door swung open. She turned back and pasted on a smile.

'There—see? All safe. Now, if you just take a right when you go out, the main road is about a hundred yards up the street. You should be able to get a cab from there.'

CHAPTER THREE

ARISTOTLE leaned nonchalantly against the wall, hands in the pockets of his trousers. At some stage since they'd left the hotel in town he'd undone his bow tie, and it hung rakishly open along with the top buttons of his shirt. Dark whorls of hair were visible, and Lucy felt weak with shock again at his bizarre behaviour. Belatedly she wondered if he might be drunk and she looked at him suspiciously. But then she recalled that, like her, he'd barely touched alcohol all evening. So if he wasn't drunk… Her belly fluttered ominously.

'I thought you said I'd never get a cab from there? Would you let me wander the mean streets of south London alone and defenceless? I can call a cab from your apartment…and I could murder a coffee…'

This man and the word *defenceless* did not belong in the same sentence. He smiled and her world tipped alarmingly for a second. Lucy had to swallow her retort, along with the stomach-churning realisation that she was being subjected to her boss's teasing and charming side. She heard the lift jerking into life again. More people arriving home from a night out. Suddenly she was terrified that it might be her very bubbly but very nosy neighbour Miranda. She could just imagine trying to explain this: a gorgeous, lounging six-foot-four

Greek tycoon in their mildew stained hallway. Her dress was suddenly the least of her worries.

'OK, fine. I'll call you a cab and get you a coffee.'

Lucy walked in and stood back to let Aristotle through. Immediately the air seemed to be sucked out of the room and replaced with his sheer dynamism. Lucy closed her door just as she heard the very drunken-sounding laughter of her neighbour and gave a sigh of relief.

As Aristotle started to prowl around her humble sitting room Lucy spied a lacy bra hanging over the chair nearest the kitchen. She dived for it while he was turned away and hurriedly balled it up. Aristotle turned round and Lucy's belly spasmed.

'Coffee,' she babbled. 'I'll get the coffee on.'

She turned and fled into the small kitchen off the sitting room and stuffed the bra into a cupboard, taking out coffee and setting the kettle to boil. She kept looking surreptitiously into the sitting room. Aristotle was still prowling around. Except now he'd taken off his jacket, and she could see the broad line of his back tapering down into an impossibly lean waist. Her gaze followed the line down over taut buttocks and long, long legs...

The shrill, piercing scream of the kettle made her jump, and she winced when drops of boiling water splashed on clumsy hands. She gathered her dress together and walked back into the sitting room, noticing that Aristotle had put on some lights. Their glow of warmth lent an intimacy to the scene that raised her blood pressure. She had the vague thought of going to get changed out of the dress, but couldn't contemplate the idea of removing a stitch of clothing while he was anywhere near. She noticed then that he was studying a photo in his hand, with a slight frown between those black brows. Lucy was terrified he might recognise the woman in the picture. She handed him the coffee, forcing him to put the picture down and take the cup.

He just gestured with his head. 'Who is that? You and your mother?'

Lucy looked down at the photo in the frame and fought the urge to snatch it out of sight. It was a favourite one of her and her mum, taken in Paris when Lucy had been about twelve. They were wrapped up against the cold, their faces close together, but even from the picture you could tell that Lucy hadn't taken after her mother's delicate red-haired beauty. She'd already been taller than her mother by then.

She nervously adjusted it slightly and replied, 'Yes,' clearly not inviting any more questions.

Aristotle looked at Lucy. She was as nervous and skittish as a foal—avoiding his eye, her hand in a white-knuckle grip on that dress. That was what had pushed him over the edge. Seeing those soft pale thighs exposed to his gaze, one long leg already out of the car. It had taken every ounce of restraint not to reach out and run his hand up the soft inner skin of one gloriously lush thigh.

Especially after an evening that had been a form of torture, trying to focus on work while she'd stood beside him. Following her out of the car and up to this apartment had felt as necessary as breathing. But now he forced himself to take a step back, sensing her extreme nervousness.

She gestured jerkily to a seat. 'Please, sit down while you have your coffee. I'll call a cab. It may take a while to come at this hour.'

Aristotle sat down on a springy couch under the window and watched as Lucy went to the phone on the other side of the room and made the call, turning her back firmly to him. He tried to bank down the intense surge of desire even her back was igniting within him and thought back to the function.

She'd been a surprisingly pleasurable and easy date,

offering intelligently insightful comments on more than one person, showing snippets of dry humour. At one point she'd caught him off-guard entirely, when she'd seamlessly switched to accentless and fluent French. He'd become accustomed to people *saying* they were multi-lingual and meaning they had the basics, like hello and goodbye. Something dark lodged in his chest. He'd also been inordinately aware of the keen male interest she'd generated and how seemingly oblivious she'd been to it. He wasn't used to that.

Fighting the sudden surge of something very primal, he let his eyes drift down over her body and long legs; a vivid image exploded into his head of the moment her dress had split. He wondered how those legs might feel wrapped around his waist as he thrust deeper and deeper into her slick heat. Arousal was immediate and uncomfortable. He shifted on the seat, and even the evident relief in Lucy's voice when she got through to the cab company did little to dampen it.

When Lucy put the phone down, she could finally turn and look her boss in the eye. Escape was imminent. She just had to make some small talk. 'Ten minutes for the cab.' She sat down gratefully in the chair beside the phone, relief making her feel weak. She was still clutching the torn dress over her legs, hanging on to it like a lifeline.

Aristotle leant forward and put down his coffee cup. He had an intense gleam in his green eyes. 'We're going to be spending a lot of time together in Athens.' He looked around her apartment, and then back to her. 'I thought this might be a good opportunity to get to know each other a little better.'

Something treacherously like disappointment rushed through Lucy, but everything within her rejected it. Had she been so blind? Had she truly suspected for a moment that Aristotle had been rushing her up here to try and make love to her? She felt very brittle all of a sudden.

'Of course. I mean, I could…' She racked her brain. Evidently she had to find some way of giving some information to Aristotle, so he didn't feel as if he had to follow her up to her apartment to talk to her. 'I could fill out a questionnaire…?'

He arched a brow.

'A personal questionnaire…if you want to get to know more…about my history.' A leaden weight made her feel heavy inside. She'd become an expert at putting a glamorous spin on her life with her mother. On her history. Glossing over the reality.

But Aristotle was shaking his head and standing up, coming towards her. He came and stood right in front of her, and Lucy realised that she was in a very vulnerable position, her eye level at his crotch. She stood too, so suddenly that she swayed, and Aristotle put out his hands to steady her. They were on her waist. Immediately it was an invasion of her space—especially when she was so self-conscious about her body.

With one hand she tried to knock him away but his hands were immovable. Her other hand was still clinging onto her dress with a death grip. She looked at him and her brain felt hot, fuzzy. He was too close. She could smell his fresh citrusy scent, mixed in with something much more male, elemental. All she could see were his eyes; all she could feel were those hands, like a brand on her body.

He was talking. She tried to concentrate on his words.

'…more along the lines of this…'

And then, as realisation exploded inside her, Aristotle's head was coming down, closer and closer. Everything went dark as his mouth covered hers, warm and firm and so exotic that she couldn't move.

It was so shocking that Lucy continued standing there like a statue. Through her mind ran the comforting words, *You won't feel anything. You're cold inside. You're not your mother.*

You don't react to this. You don't crave men…sex… You've proved this to yourself…

But, as if disconnected from her mind, a radiating heat was taking over, spreading upwards from a very secret part of her. A core she'd never acknowledged before. A core that had never been touched.

Aristotle was pulling her closer. Those big hands were still around her waist, spanning it now, fingers digging into soft, yielding flesh. He was warm and firm, and as he brought her flush against his body she realised just how hard he was. How tall, and how strong. He was huge, and she had the distinct impression for the first time in her life of being…somehow delicate. No one had ever made her feel like that.

He moved one of his hands upwards from her waist, skimming close to her breast which tingled in reaction, the peak tightening almost painfully. But then he speared that hand through her hair, around the back of her head, angling her towards him more. She was aware of the rush of disappointment that his hand hadn't lingered, cupped the weight of her breast.

His mouth was insistent, but something inside Lucy was like ice amidst the heat, still protecting her from fully feeling. It was a wall of defence she'd erected over a long time…and yet even as she thought that she suddenly visualised that defence crumbling.

As sensation got stronger, igniting an alien urgency, panic surged. Aristotle could have no idea of what was happening inside her, how cataclysmic her reaction was, but at that moment he took his head away and looked down into her wide eyes. Somewhere Lucy was dimly aware that she wasn't pushing him away…which she could. But she felt so heavy, so deliciously lethargic, and she couldn't think when he was so close and looking deep into her eyes like this.

He said gutturally, 'Lucy…I can feel you holding back. You're shaking with it.'

And then she became aware that she *was* shaking—like a leaf, all over. Reality exploded around her. She was in her boss's arms and he was kissing her! The feelings rippling through her were intense to the point of overwhelming her completely, more intoxicating than anything she'd ever experienced, or thought she could experience. With that thought sanity tried to break through: she didn't respond to kissing in this way. And yet…she was.

Aristotle chose that moment to kiss her again, and Lucy was caught between two worlds, defenceless and vulnerable, conflicting desires whirling in her head, making her dizzy. Making her weak against this far too seductive attack on her senses. One hand was curled against Aristotle's chest, and as his mouth moved over hers once again her fingers unfurled, like the petals of a flower opening to the sun. When his tongue traced along the seam of her tightly closed mouth the sensation made her open her lips minutely, some dark and distant part of her wanting this, wanting to experience this, and Aristotle took immediate advantage, opening her mouth, forcing her to accept him. And to respond.

When his tongue-tip touched hers it set off a chain reaction in her body. Suddenly she was *feeling* for the first time, and it was too strong to resist—like a flash-flood carrying her downstream. She moved closer to Aristotle's body and felt his growl of approval. His tongue stabbed deep, exploring and coaxing hers to touch and taste. The hand at her waist brought her even closer, and the evidence of his arousal pressing into her soft belly elicited a deep craving feeling not of disgust, but of desire to experience *union*.

Her fingers tangled in surprisingly silky hair; she could feel her back arch wantonly towards him. He shaped the indent of her waist and hips and Lucy didn't feel self-conscious, she felt exultant. When his hands moved to cup her buttocks and pull her even tighter into the cradle of his lap her breath caught.

Aristotle tore his mouth away and looked down at her. Their bodies were still plastered together. Their breath came swift and uneven, and he didn't take his eyes off hers as he reached one hand down between them and found where her hand was still tightly clenched over the rent sides of the dress. He loosened her fingers and, helpless, Lucy could only look deep into his glittering eyes as she felt the dress fall apart and his hand smooth up over her thigh, then between her legs, climbing higher and higher.

He was looking at her. His eyes were on her…studying her. While his hand—

'You're so beautiful. Why do you hide yourself away, Lucy?'

It wasn't his hand climbing to such an intimate place but his words that broke her out of her sensual stasis: *so beautiful…*

She wasn't beautiful. She'd heard those words a million times before. Not directed at her—never at her. But at someone else. Someone who had craved them; someone who had spent her life being defined by men's opinion of her.

The shock of everything suddenly hit her, and made Lucy jerk back violently, knocking his hand away and pulling her dress together again. She had the mortifying image in her head of wantonly pressing as close as she could, and the shame of her reaction to that made her feel nauseous. Between her legs she throbbed and tingled.

Her voice was shaking and thin, too high. 'This is completely inappropriate. I'm your *assistant.*'

Aristotle's face was uncharacteristically flushed. 'You're also the one woman I can't stop thinking about and wanting. And it's a bit late to put on the injured virgin act.'

He raked a hand through his hair in frustration, leaving it gorgeously unruly.

Lucy shook her head in rejection of that, trying to ignore the way her mouth felt so full and plump. She felt anything but virginal right now. In a few seconds he'd managed to blast to smithereens the knowledge that she'd comforted herself with ever since she *had* lost her virginity: she was frigid.

'No. I'm your assistant. This is not possible.' More shame rushed through her as she said, 'If you think I gave you some indication that I might welcome…' She couldn't even say it. 'You're just…bored or something. You can't possibly—'

'Can't I?' he interrupted harshly. He stood with hands fisted at his sides and glowered at her. 'I saw you changing the other morning and I felt like a schoolboy watching a naked woman for the first time. No woman has ever reduced me to that. And you want me too, Lucy. You've just shown me that.'

Embarrassment washed through her in a wave of heat. He *had* seen her. She'd known it…but to hear him confirm it nearly made her mind short-circuit. And along with the embarrassment came another feeling, one of illicit pleasure, when she remembered seeing his face. She shook her head again, even fiercer this time, both hands clutching the dress.

Just at that moment the phone rang shrilly. Lucy jumped. She was starting to shake; reaction was setting in. 'That's the taxi. Get out right now.' When he didn't move she said, *'Please.'*

Aristotle finally strode over to pick up his coat and, flinging it over one shoulder, he walked to the door. He looked back at her for a long moment, hugely imposing and dark in her plain little apartment. Men like him weren't meant for scenes like this, she thought.

The phone had stopped, but now started again.

'I'll see you on Monday, Lucy. This isn't over—not by a long shot.'

And then he was gone. Lucy stood stock still and could barely breathe. When the phone impacted upon her consciousness again she went over and picked it up. 'He's on his way down,' she said.

When she was certain he had gone, Lucy undressed and had a steaming hot shower, thinking perhaps it might eradicate the painfully intense feelings Aristotle had aroused in her when he'd touched her and looked at her. She dressed in her oldest and comfiest pyjamas and made herself a hot chocolate, dislodging the bra she'd hurriedly hidden as she did so from the cupboard. Heat rose upwards again, but she resolutely ignored it and went into the sitting room and sank onto the couch, cradling the hot cup in cold hands.

She reached up and took down the photo of her and her mother and tears filled her eyes as emotion surged upwards. She felt incredibly raw after what had just happened.

Her mother had been diagnosed with early onset Alzheimer's two years ago. It had come on the back of her growing ever more forgetful and irritable, prone to mood swings and dramatics. It had been so unlike her usually sanguine mother that Lucy had insisted she go to be checked out by a doctor. They'd run some tests, and as soon as a diagnosis had been made her mother's condition had worsened by the day—almost as if naming it had allowed it to take hold completely.

At first Lucy had been able to look after her in their small townhouse near Holland Park, but when she'd come home one day to find her mother wailing inconsolably in a flooded kitchen, with all the gas rings of the cooker on and alight and no idea how or why she'd done it, Lucy had known she couldn't fight it on her own any more.

She'd started with home help—the cost of which had rapidly eaten up all their savings. Her mother had never worried about money too much beyond making sure Lucy was provided for, and there had invariably been a new rich lover more than happy to provide. However, in recent years Lucy's mother had been coming to terms with the harsh realities of aging in a world where youth and beauty were a more potent draw to powerful men. The protection of rich lovers had all but disappeared.

Lucy's mouth compressed as her finger ran over her mother's image in the picture. She supposed in the nineteenth century her mother might have been considered one of the most famous courtesans of her time. But in this lifetime she'd been a famous and much sought after burlesque dancer—a true artist. Lucy's mouth tightened even more; her mother had simply got used to the attention of very rich, very powerful men.

She'd craved the control she'd had over them—her ability to reduce them to ardent lovers, desperate to please her in any way they could. Her allure and beauty had been legendary. Her powerful lovers had funded their lives, and unwittingly helped put Lucy through the best schools all over the world. She couldn't denigrate her mother's memory now by judging her over where that money had come from. Her mother had simply used all the tools at her disposal to survive.

Her father had been one of those men. When he'd found out Maxine was pregnant and refusing to give up her baby, he'd paid some maintenance but hadn't wanted anything to do with Lucy. When Lucy was sixteen he'd died, and maintenance had stopped abruptly—because of course he hadn't told his family about her.

What had upset Lucy more than anything else was the lack of confidence and self-esteem her mother had suffered that only she, as her daughter, had been privy to. While on the one hand her mother had been in control, using those men as they used her, on another, much more vulnerable level she had craved their affection and approval. She'd used her beauty to enthral her lovers, but she'd been broken in two every time they'd walked away, leaving behind nothing but costly gems, clothes—*things.*

It had been shortly after finding her mother so distraught in the flooded kitchen that Lucy had discovered the house they'd lived in—a generous present from another lover—had never been signed over to her mother, despite assurances at the time. The man was a prominent politician who'd just died. Lucy's mother's solicitor had advised that Lucy should not contest ownership of the house when the family had discovered its existence, as obviously they had no idea of their father's secret affair. The family had debts to clear on the death of their father, and Lucy had had no option but to let the house go. The precariousness of their situation had forged within Lucy a deep desire for order and her own financial independence.

About a year ago they'd moved into her current small apartment. Lucy had still hoped that home help would be enough, but the cost of it had barely left her with enough to buy food at the end of each week. Her job at Levakis Enterprises was the only thing that kept them afloat. And now with her increase in wages, it was the only thing giving her mum the opportunity to have decent care.

Lucy stared unseeingly down at the picture, and suddenly an image broke through—Aristotle standing right here in this room, holding her close, his hand between her legs. She could remember the way she'd throbbed and burned for that hand to go even higher, to where she ached. *To where she still ached.* Lucy shifted so violently in reaction that the picture fell from her lap to the wooden floor and the glass smashed in the frame. With a cry of dismay she put down her cup and picked it up carefully. As she did so, something hard solidified in her chest.

She knew exactly how to handle this situation, how to

handle Aristotle Levakis and make sure everything returned to normal. She couldn't contemplate how her decision would impact her mother just yet. All she knew was that she had to protect herself—because she'd never felt under such threat in her life. She would make sure her mother was safe and cared for. *She would.* She just couldn't do it like this.

On Monday morning, early, Ari stood at the window of his huge office, with its commanding view out over the city of London and all its impressive spires and rooftops. From the moment he'd been placed in charge of Levakis Enterprises at the age of twenty-seven, on the death of his father five years previously, he'd moved the power centre of the business here to London, his adopted home.

He'd told himself it was for strategic reasons, and certainly the business had thrived and grown exponentially since he'd moved it here, but it was also a very distinct gesture from him to his family, to say *he* was in control, not them. They'd shunned him enough over the years. No way was he going to play happy families back in Athens. And while he had left the original office there, which his half-brother now oversaw, they all knew that it was just a symbolic front for the business. Ari controlled its beating heart, and it lay here, under the grey and rain-soaked skies of London.

But today his main focus was not on business; it was on something much more personal and closer to home. On something so exquisitely feminine and alluring that he didn't know how he'd managed to control himself for the past weekend and not go back to that small dingy apartment, knock down the door and take Lucy hard and fast, before she could draw up that *faux* injured virgin response again. He could still feel the imprint of every womanly curve as he'd held her close to his body. She'd been more lusciously voluptuous than any fantasy he could have had.

His hands were clenched to fists deep in his pockets now, and his jaw was gritted hard against the unwelcome surging of desire. His assistant was causing him frustration of the most strategic kind.

She wanted him. And he couldn't understand where her reticence came from. No woman was reticent with him; he saw, he desired, he took. It was quite simple and always had been. An alien and uncomfortable feeling nagged him as he acknowledged the dominant feeling he'd had the other night. He'd felt *ruthless* as he'd coaxed and cajoled a response from Lucy. When she'd finally capitulated, even for that brief moment, it had been a sweeter conquest than any victory he could remember. He didn't usually associate ruthlessness with women—that was reserved for business—and the fact that such a base emotion was spilling over into his personal life was—

Ari heard a noise come from the outer office—Lucy's office—and his body tensed with a frisson of anticipation, all previous thoughts scattered to the winds.

He wanted Lucy Proctor and she would pay for making him desire her by giving herself up to him, wholly and without reservation, until he was sated and could move back into the circles in which he belonged. He vowed this now, as he heard a sharp knock on his door, and waited for a moment before turning around, schooling his features and saying with quiet, yet forceful emphasis, 'Come.'

Lucy took a deep breath outside the heavy oak door. As soon as she heard that deeply autocratic *'Come'* her nerves jangled and her heart started racing. Just before she opened the door, her hand clammy and slippy on the round knob, she prayed that the make-up she'd put on that morning would hide the dark circles under her eyes. She hadn't slept a wink all weekend.

Steeling herself like never before, she opened the door and stepped in. Aristotle was standing with his hands in his pockets and his back to the huge window. Waves of virile masculinity seemed to radiate from him and Lucy's throat went dry. For an awful second her mind seemed to go blank and be replaced with nothing but heat...but as her hand clenched on the envelope she gave an inward sigh of relief and reminded herself that she'd soon be out of this man's disturbing orbit.

She walked further into the office and tried to ignore the way Aristotle's narrowed gaze on her was making her even more nervous. She came to a halt just a few feet from the desk.

She cleared her throat. 'Sir, I...' Heat washed into her face. 'That is...Aristotle...' She stopped. She was already a gibbering wreck.

'I thought I told you there was no need for you to wear your glasses.'

Lucy's hand went reflexively to touch the sturdy frames. She cursed herself for having told him she didn't need them, and bristled at his high-handed manner. The sharp edge of the envelope reassured her.

'Well, I feel more comfortable wearing them. The fact is that—'

'Well, I don't.' He was curt, abrupt. 'You work for *me*, and I don't want to see them again. And you can also stop tying your hair back as if you're doing some kind of religious penance.'

Lucy gasped. She could feel the colour washing out of her face, only to be swiftly replaced by mortified heat.

Knowing that she had nothing to lose, she didn't curb her tongue, but her voice when it came was slightly strangled. 'Is there anything else you'd like to comment on while you're at it?'

Aristotle leaned back against the window and negligently crossed one ankle over the other, crossed his arms over that formidable chest. His eyes took on a slumberous quality that made Lucy's breath falter and a tight coil of sensation burn down low in her belly.

'Have you thrown out that skirt yet?'

Lucy's hands clenched. She didn't feel the edges of the envelope any more, or remember what she was here to do. Right now she was being subjected to the lazy appraisal of a man who, she told herself, was just like every other man who had traipsed in and out of her mother's life. The fact that her predominant emotion wasn't the anger she'd expected made her feel very vulnerable.

'It's none of your business where that blasted skirt is. You can rest assured that you won't have to be subjected to seeing me wear it again, because I'm here to—'

'That's a pity.'

Lucy's mouth was still open on the unfinished part of her sentence. She blinked as his words sank in. She shook her head. She had to have misheard. Distracted, and hating herself for it, she asked, 'What did you say?'

He stood then, and even though he didn't come towards her she took a step back.

'I said, that's a pity. You'd be surprised how much of my mental energy that skirt has been taking up. I think I may have been too hasty in my judgement of it.'

Lucy shook her head again and could feel herself trembling inwardly. She felt as if she were in some twilight zone. What about the Augustine Archers of the world, impeccably groomed to within an inch of their skinny designer lives? Surely he couldn't really mean that he preferred…? Her mind shut down at that, but the words slipped out and she watched herself as if from a distance as she said faintly, 'But…it was just a high street skirt that shrank in the wash. I didn't have time to get a new one. You thought it was inappropriate enough to have me taken to task for it.'

'That was a mistake.' His eyes flicked down over her body, and Lucy's flesh tingled as if he'd touched her. Even though she wore perfectly fitting and respectable trousers, a high-necked shirt and a jacket, she felt undressed.

When his eyes rose to meet hers again she registered the dangerous gleam in their depths. The bubble of unreality burst. Self-preservation was back. The envelope. She held it out now, with a none too steady hand.

Aristotle looked from her face down to it and then back up. He arched an enquiring brow.

Lucy stammered, 'It's—it's my letter…of resignation.'

Ari's hands clenched. Something surged through his body—a primal need not to let this woman go. No way was she walking out of here. That ruthless feeling was back.

He shook his head. 'No, it's not.'

'Yes, it is,' Lucy replied automatically, a little perplexed.

'No. It's not.'

Anger started to lick upwards as it dawned on Lucy that this wasn't going to be the quick result she'd hoped for.

'Yes, Mr Levakis, it is. Please accept my resignation with the grace with which it's tendered.' She held out the envelope further. 'I am not available for…extra services outside work, and your behaviour the other night was not acceptable.'

Lucy's eyes had turned to a dark slate-grey and they were flashing. There was a resolute tilt to her chin. Ari marvelled that he hadn't noticed it before now, but this woman had passion oozing from every pore of her tightly held body. She had backbone. Far from fading into the background, as he'd so misguidedly believed her to have done from day one, she'd been there under his nose the whole time. He could see now that her appeal had been working on him subliminally, bringing him to the point he had now reached: the point of no return, unless this woman was with him.

Ari moved around the desk and perched on the edge, arms

still folded. When he saw Lucy's eyes flick betrayingly down to his thighs he smiled inwardly, and smiled even more when he saw a flush stain her cheeks. *How* had he ever though of her as plain or unassuming? He ignored her outstretched hand and the white envelope.

Lucy refused to show how intimidated she was by moving back, but she wanted to—desperately. Her breath was coming in shallow bursts. She felt as if she wanted to reach up and undo the top button of her blouse.

Aristotle cocked his head and asked enquiringly, with a small frown, 'Now, exactly what part of the other night would you say was not acceptable?' He answered himself. 'The part where I escorted you safely to your door? Or perhaps the part where I accepted the coffee you made me?'

Lucy's other hand balled into a fist and she bit out, 'You know exactly what I'm talking about.'

His face cleared, the frown disappeared and he said, 'Ah! You mean the part where I proved just how mutual our attraction is?'

CHAPTER FOUR

LUCY flushed even hotter, mortified heat drenching her in an upward sweep. Much to her utter humiliation she knew it wasn't *all* mortification. Some of it was pure...*thrill*. This man was doing nothing short of creating a nuclear reaction within her, comprehensively threatening everything she'd protected herself with for years.

She dropped her outstretched hand without even realising what she was doing and shook her head, finally taking a step back, pretending she wasn't as affected as she was as if her life depended on it.

'You mean the part where you mauled me? That wasn't mutual attraction.'

Immediately he tensed, and his eyes flashed dangerously. Lucy swallowed. She knew she'd just said the worst thing possible. Most bosses in this situation would sense the potential danger of having a sexual harassment suit landed against them and back off. But Aristotle Levakis was not most bosses, and Lucy guessed belatedly that no woman, *ever*, had accused him of mauling them. Certainly her dreams over the weekend hadn't been of someone mauling her—quite the opposite, in fact.

Aristotle stood to his full height, power and pure sexual charisma bouncing off him in affronted waves. He arched a brow, his arms still folded tightly across his chest, the biceps of his arms bunching even through the material of his silk shirt.

'*Mauled*?' he repeated softly, dangerously.

Lucy swallowed again, her throat suddenly as dry as parchment. She nodded, but felt herself curling up inside with humiliation.

Aristotle came and stood very close Lucy had to tip her head back and look up. She clenched her jaw. He was looking down at her with an expressionless face, those light green eyes glittering. Dark slashes of colour highlighted his cheekbones. He was livid, she recognised, and a flutter of fear came low in her belly, along with another flutter of something much more dangerous.

He started to walk around her. Lucy held herself rigid.

From behind her she heard him say, 'When I put my hands on your waist you didn't stop me or push me away.'

'I—' She began, but stopped as the memory of his hands on her waist speared through her. How his fingers had dug into her soft flesh. How she'd wanted them to dig harder.

'Then, when I kissed you, you also didn't pull away.' His voice was low and sultry. 'I know when a woman is enjoying being kissed, *moro mou*, believe me.'

He was still behind her, and Lucy was finding it increasingly difficult to concentrate. His voice was so hypnotic, resonating with something that pulled on her insides and left her weak.

'I...I...didn't like it.'

'Liar.' It came so softly from close behind her head that she jumped minutely, her skin breaking into goosebumps.

He moved to her side. Lucy fought against closing her eyes and wondered dimly why she just didn't walk away, but she knew on some level that she was afraid if she moved she might fall down. She stayed rigid.

'You did like it…when my tongue touched yours…when you let me explore the sweetness of that mouth. Did I tell you that I'm fascinated by the gap in your teeth? Right now all I want to do is kiss you again until you're so boneless in my arms that all I'd have to do is carry you to the couch over there…'

Lucy's breath had stopped. Her brain had certainly stopped functioning. The couch was in her peripheral vision, and Aristotle was right in front of her again. For a big man, he moved as silently as a panther.

She closed her eyes in a childish gesture to block him out, but quickly realised what a mistake that was when he continued, 'I'd lay you down and remove those glasses and let your hair out of its tight confinement…'

At that moment Lucy's head throbbed unmercifully, as if in league with him.

'Then I'd start to undo your buttons, one by one, but I probably wouldn't be able to resist kissing you again, coaxing you to bite down on me too, so you could feel how I might taste.'

The sensation of what it might be like to bite into the sensual curve of his lower lip was shockingly vivid. Lucy was starting to quiver badly now. Her eyes still closed tight, she felt hot and flushed all over, and between her legs… Her mind seized.

'Stop…' she said threadily. 'Please…'

'But you see you wouldn't want me to stop, as your shirt fell apart, baring those gorgeous breasts to my gaze… Is the lace of your bra chafing you now, Lucy? Are your nipples tight and tingling? Aching for my touch? Aching for my mouth? I would take those peaks and suck them into my mouth, hard, until they're aroused to the point of pain. And then I'd cover your body with mine, so that you could feel how turned-on I am. *Even right now* I'd lift up your leg and let my hand slide over the silk of your stocking, all the way to the soft pale flesh of your thigh. You'd be moaning softly, willing my hand even higher, to that secret place between your legs where you're aching for me to find the silk of your pants drenched with desire. You'd beg for me to slide them aside so that I could feel for myself—'

'Stop!' Lucy's eyes flew open and in an instant she was jerking away—only realising at the last second that he wasn't even holding her. He held up his hands to prove the point. Her breath was coming in short, shallow gasps, her breasts felt heavy, their tips tight and tingling, exactly as he'd described, and between her legs seemed to burn a molten pool of something dangerous and unwelcome... It was that that had finally woken her out of this awful, *delicious* dream.

But it wasn't delicious—it *wasn't*, she told herself desperately as she looked anywhere but at Aristotle. She felt disorientated, dizzy, as if she could almost believe she *had* been on that couch. Her upper lip felt moist. Her hands clenched and she realised that she no longer held the envelope. In that instant she saw that it was in one of his hands and he was ripping it in two.

She put out a hand. 'Wait! What are you doing?'

Lucy also realised, along with everything else in that moment, that contrary to her own state of near collapse Aristotle looked cool, calm and collected—a million miles away from the man who had been just whispering in her ear how *aroused* he was. She was a quivering wreck and he hadn't even touched her.

His cool voice cut through her like a knife as she watched him turn on his heel and walk back around his desk. 'I'm putting this letter of resignation where it belongs—in the bin.' And he promptly did just that.

Lucy was a mess, still reeling from the way his voice and words had affected her, and how utterly unaffected he clearly was. He was sitting behind his desk now, for all the world as if nothing had just happened, and as if he was waiting for her to sit and take notes.

'Mr Levakis—'

His voice was curt. 'We've been through this before. I told you to call me Aristotle. I don't want to tell you again.'

Lucy all but exploded. 'I am resigning. There is nothing you can do or say to stop me. I will not stay and be subjected to the kind of treatment you just…just subjected me to.'

Aristotle was looking down, flicking through papers, and he said easily, 'Lucy, I didn't even have to touch you to turn you on, so when the time comes and I do touch you for real can you imagine how good it's going to be? Why would you deny yourself that?'

For a million and one good reasons! Lucy saw red spots dance before her eyes. His words had impacted upon her so deep, and in a place so visceral, she nearly screamed with frustration. But she swallowed it down and said, as coolly and calmly as she could, 'It's clear that your arrogance is clouding your ability to assimilate this information. Perhaps it'll become more clear once I've gone. I can send you another copy of my resignation. Good day, Mr Levakis.'

She turned on her heel and was almost at the door when she heard him, deadly soft. 'If you walk through that door, Lucy Proctor, you'll be hearing from my lawyers within the hour.'

Lucy stopped in her tracks, her hand still in the act of reaching for the doorknob. She turned around slowly and saw that hard green gaze spearing her on the spot. Her stomach felt as if she was in freefall off a huge cliff.

'What are you talking about?' But dread was already trickling through her as her professional brain went into overdrive and she had a sickening memory of signing that other contract along with the one for her job. She really hadn't thought this through with her usual clear rationality at all.

'Well, for a start, you're obliged to give me at least four weeks' notice, as per your standard work contract, and if you leave before the merger is completed you'll be sued. It's quite simple.'

And utterly devastating…Lucy realised with mounting horror.

He sat back in his chair. 'We leave for Athens in a week. You know far too much, and have been privy to all the top secret discussions. Quite apart from that, if you left now you'd be leaving me without an assistant for the most important joining between two Greek companies in years. That is something I will not allow to happen. If it means I have to threaten you with legal action to get you to stay then so be it. I won't hesitate to use the full force of my power.'

He sat forward then, and he had never looked so intimidating. 'Lucy, I don't think I need to tell you that your career would be comprehensively ruined if you insist on leaving. You could be crippled financially for years.'

Lucy wasn't sure how she remained standing. She'd known all this—she'd *known*. She'd been smart enough to read the fine print of both contracts, and at the time it had given her a sense of security to know that Levakis wouldn't be able to turn around and get rid of her at a moment's notice. It was what had given her the confidence to put her mum in that home— the confidence to go to the bank and take out a loan which would assure her mother's place in that home for at least a year. Lucy had known that as long as she could keep up the payments everything would be secure for the short term, and hopefully for the long-term future.

But now…if she walked out of here and incurred Aristotle Levakis' wrath she'd be kissing all that goodbye. She could well imagine the loan from the bank being called in. Losing her job would quickly mean that she'd have no source of income with which to pay for her mum's accommodation. She'd be back to square one, becoming the primary carer, and without a job that would be impossible.

She said now, in a small voice, 'You would do that…' It wasn't a question.

'Without a doubt,' he answered grimly. 'This merger and this company are too important to me. They are everything.'

So what am, I then? Lucy wondered a little wildly. Just a convenient plaything because you happen to be bored with all the usual sycophants?

He stood again then, but Lucy was in too much shock and distress to move as he came closer, hands in his pockets. He looked smug. He knew he had her effectively trapped. Suddenly she longed to have no responsibilities, so she could just disappear. But she did, and she couldn't.

He stopped a few feet away and looked at her. Her world had been reduced to this room, this man and those eyes. And that voice.

'Lucy, I don't want to be ruthless about this, and I certainly don't relish the thought of taking action against you. I want the merger, yes, and I'll do whatever I need to to protect it and make it happen. But I also want *you*, and I will do whatever I need to in order to make that happen too.'

Lucy shook her head dumbly, even now fighting. It made something in Aristotle's eyes flash dangerously. She had thought that someone like him would give up when faced with obstinate resistance, although that assertion was now fast losing ground. She had to acknowledge that he'd most likely rarely, if ever, faced resistance from any woman.

'You've made it quite clear that it is impossible for me to leave.'

That was the understatement of the year. Her conscience mocked her. She should have realised all this at the weekend, but he'd had her head in such a tizzy all she'd been able to think of was getting away from him. She realised now that if she had thought it through she could have done her best to keep him at arm's length for the duration of the merger and *then* given her notice—instead of these dramatics, which were so unlike her.

'I'll stay for the merger and then I'll be giving you my notice.'

She would just have to worry about her mother when that happened. She hated the fact that she wasn't strong enough to try and stay and resist this man indefinitely.

Aristotle just looked at her for a long, heated moment. Lucy saw a muscle throb in his temple and it made her insides quiver like jelly. He reached out a hand and cupped her jaw. Shock and instant heat paralysed her at his touch.

'Say what you want, Lucy, if it makes you feel better, but know this: we *will* be lovers. It's as inevitable as the inclement English weather. There's something raw and singularly powerful between us and I've no intention of letting you go—either in the boardroom or in the bedroom.'

Lucy swallowed painfully. His hand still cupped her jaw, his thumb moving lazily against the sensitive skin under her chin. One thing was certain: if, in some parallel universe, she actually gave in to this man, she had no doubt that far from being given the luxury of giving notice *he'd* be the one saying goodbye—and so fast that her head would be spinning. Something like four weeks' notice would be reduced to a mocking sham of a professional nicety.

She hated the fact that it was the thought of *that* right now that made her feel more vulnerable than even the prospect of the battle to come. One other thing was sure: with every bone and last breath in her body she would resist the seduction of this man. Yet, she had to ask herself inwardly, for someone who prided herself on being frigid, why did it suddenly seem like such an uphill struggle?

A week later.

Lucy sat opposite Aristotle on his private jet as it winged its way to Athens from a stormy London. She could almost believe for a moment that she'd imagined what had happened in his office last week, when he'd declared so implacably that he was determined to have her in his bed.

Since that day when she'd been so firmly put back in her place, her letter of resignation torn up, Aristotle had been utterly consumed with business and preparations for the merger. They'd worked late into the night almost every night, and she'd been in the office most mornings as the cleaners were still finishing up. She'd never been so tired, yet so contentedly exhausted. Despite her trepidation at the undercurrents flowing under the surface, professionally speaking she'd never worked at such a heady pace, nor been entrusted with so much responsibility. The sense of pitting her wits against Aristotle and keeping up with him was exhilarating. She blocked out the snide voice that mocked her with the assertion that *work* was the only exhilarating thing.

Thankfully she hadn't had time for much more than falling into bed, snatching some food, and getting up again. The weekend had been a blur of last-minute visits to the office, packing, and a bittersweet visit to her mum, before she'd been collected by Aristotle's driver that Sunday afternoon. The visit to her mother had been bittersweet because she'd had one of her brief lucid moments, recognising Lucy as soon she'd walked into the private room at the home.

'Lucy, darling!'

Lucy had had to swallow back a lump as she'd watched her

still beautifully elegant mother rise out of her chair by the window to greet her with her usual warm and tactile affection. Lucy had missed it so much. On Maxine's good days, and obviously this was one, she took care of her appearance. On her bad days Lucy would come in and, if not for the care of the attentive staff, her mother could look as unkempt as a bag lady. It made her heart ache with sadness as her mother had always been so fastidious about her looks.

Lucy had been careful not to let the emotion overwhelm her; these moments of lucidity were growing further and further apart, and she'd have her mother with her for only ten minutes before the inevitable decline came. The sentences would stop and falter, her eyes grow opaque, until finally she'd come to look at Lucy with a completely blank expression and say, 'I'm sorry, dear, who are you?'

It broke Lucy's heart to know that there was no point in even trying to explain where she was going, or that she was going to be out of the country for a few weeks. At least she could give thanks for the sterling round-the-clock care she could now afford. It made her attempt to resign from her job seem all the more childishly impetuous now. How could she jeopardise her mother's security? And yet how could she keep working for Aristotle once this merger was completed?

'*Lucy.*'

Lucy's head jerked round from where she'd been looking out of the window at the sea far below. Aristotle must have called her a couple of times; she could hear impatience lacing his voice. He was looking at her sternly, and at that moment Lucy realised how little space was between them—just a small table. Even as she thought that she felt Aristotle flex a leg and it brushed hers. She froze, all that heat and awareness rushing back, mocking her for believing it might have disappeared under a pile of work.

'I'm sorry. I was just thinking about something.'

He quirked a brow. 'Something more interesting than me? Or this merger? Not possible, surely.'

Lucy froze even more, she couldn't handle Aristotle when he was being like this…flirty. Yet with a steel edge. She couldn't imagine him ever being truly light, free and easy. Smiling. He was too driven, intense.

She smiled brittlely, determined that he shouldn't see his effect. 'Of course not. How could I?'

At that moment the steward arrived to serve them lunch. Lucy automatically went to clear the table and her hands brushed against Aristotle's. She flinched back but tried to mask her reaction, a flush rising up over her chest. It would appear their tenuous 'work truce' had ended. Tension was a tight cord between them.

Lucy studied her food, a delicious-looking Greek salad and fresh crusty bread.

'Would you like some wine?'

She looked up to automatically shake her head. Wine on a plane with this man was a recipe for disaster.

'Some water will be fine, thanks.'

She watched as Aristotle's lean dark hand elegantly poured himself wine, and then water for her. She muttered thanks and took a deep gulp, hoping it might dampen the flames that were licking inside her.

They ate companionably in silence. It was one of the things that perplexed her about this man. They had moments like this when she could almost imagine that they might be *friends*. She'd noticed in general that he didn't feel the need to fill silences with inane chatter, and neither did she. It surprised her to find that in common. In all honesty, if it wasn't for the great hulking elephant in the room, Lucy had to admit that so far she'd enjoyed working for Aristotle and admired his work ethic.

She was finishing her final mouthful of salad when she

sensed him leaning back in his chair. She could feel the brush of his leg against hers again and fought not to move it aside. She was aware of his regard and it made her self-conscious.

'You really don't approve of me, Lucy, do you?'

She looked up, surprised. It was the last thing she would have imagined hearing him say. She gulped and wiped her mouth with a napkin, a flare of guilt assailing her.

'I…I don't think one way or the other. I'm here as your assistant, not to form a personal opinion.' She wondered wildly what had brought this on.

He folded his arms across his chest, supremely at ease.

'I've seen those little looks you dart at me—those little looks that have me all summed up. And when I asked you to send a gift to Augustine Archer, you most certainly didn't approve of that.'

Lucy was so tense now she thought she might crack. 'Like I said before…it's not my place to judge—'

'And yet you do,' he inserted silkily.

Lucy's face flamed. Yes, she did. She had him wrapped up, parcelled and boxed as being exactly like the men she'd seen court her mother, and no matter how she'd seen him treat women, the inherently unfair judgement of that made her feel unaccountably guilty all of a sudden.

It goaded her into saying, 'All right. Fine. I don't think it was particularly professional of you to ask me to send a parting gift to your mistress. It's not my business, it made me uncomfortable, and I felt that it crossed the boundaries.' *Not to mention that it made me feel angry and disappointed too.* But Lucy held her tongue. She couldn't go that far, and those revelations made her feel far too vulnerable.

She felt as prim as a mother superior, and couldn't look Aristotle in the eye, sure he had to be laughing his head off at her.

'You're right. I won't ask you to do that again.'

She looked at him in shock. His face wasn't creased in hilarity, it was stone cold sober.

'To be honest, Lucy, I did it to get a reaction out of you…and you gave it to me.'

She frowned and shook her head minutely. 'But why?'

He shrugged one broad shoulder nonchalantly, not at all put out to be discussing this, his gaze on hers not wavering for a second. 'Because I sensed something about you, under the surface…' His gaze dropped to where she could feel her breasts rising and falling with her breath. He looked back up and her heart stopped. 'And I suddenly realised that you were causing me an inordinate amount of…frustration.' His mouth tightened. 'I blamed you for the fact that it had become necessary to say goodbye to a perfectly good mistress.'

His words caused little short of an explosion of reaction within Lucy. She tried desperately to block it out—the realisation that even then—Her brain froze at that implication. Her hands clenched tight on the table and she hid them on her lap.

'Look, Aristotle…' She knew she was all but begging. 'I've already told you, I'm not interested in anything…like that. Really, I'm not. If I've given you that impression I'm really sorry.'

His eyes flashed and he leaned forward, hands on the table, starkly brown against the surface. 'Don't patronise me. You give me that impression every time you look at me. It's there right now. You're desperately aware of where my leg is—how close it is to yours under this table—'

'Stop it,' Lucy all but cried out. 'Don't do that words thing again.' She wouldn't be able to handle it.

Triumph lit Aristotle's eyes. 'See? You want me, Lucy. I can smell it from here. But don't worry. I'm not some lecherous boss who is going to force you into some compromising position. You'll come to me. It's just a matter of time before we see how long you can hold out against it.'

Between Lucy's thighs she felt indecently damp. She coloured even more hotly. Could he really smell that? Did desire have a smell? And since when had she admitted it *was* desire and not just sheer banal human reaction? The thought made her squirm, but also made her feel weak and achy. She scrambled out of her seat. She had to get away.

As she pushed past his chair he snaked out a hand and caught her wrist. She looked down, and he was looking right up at her, trapping her. She watched as he took her wrist and brought it to his mouth. He pressed his lips against the sensitive skin on the underside. And then she felt his tongue flick out to taste her there, right against her pulse. With a strangled cry that spoke more of desire than disgust, she yanked her hand away and ran, aiming for the toilet at the back, his mocking chuckle following her all the way. Any complacency she'd felt in the past week was blown sky-high to smithereens. He'd just been biding his time.

She locked herself in with shaking hands and looked at herself in the small, unforgiving mirror. She had to fatally and finally accept the knowledge that she desired this man. It wasn't just his indisputable charisma, it was *him*. And his effect on *her*. She wanted him with a hunger that she'd always intellectualised as something she'd never experience. Except now she was. And it was ten million times worse than anything she could have ever imagined.

This was nothing short of catastrophic when she'd happily devoted herself to a life that had promised to offer up only the sort of passion she could handle. Safe, staid, unexciting. She hadn't committed herself to being celibate—she did hope to one day meet someone and settle down, perhaps even have children—but at no point had she ever hoped for the kind of fulfilment that was a deep throbbing ache within her right now.

She'd unconsciously left her hair loose, and now she

bundled it up again, tight, digging out some hairpins from her pocket to hold it in place. Then she searched for and found the comforting frames of her glasses. She'd kept them close by but hadn't worn them all week, as she'd been genuinely afraid of what Aristotle might do, but now she needed to send him a message once and for all. Lucy Proctor was not available and not interested. And never would be. If she told herself that enough, she might actually believe it.

Even though Aristotle might be laughing at Lucy's reaction, his body most certainly wasn't laughing. His body had never felt so serious and intent on one thing: carnal satisfaction, and with that woman. He burned from head to toe with it. The past week had been pure torture. They'd worked in such close proximity that it had taken all of his strength and will-power not to sweep aside the paperwork, throw her across his desk and take her there and then.

The only thing holding him back—apart from the very real need to prepare for the merger, and it irked him that that hadn't been enough—had been Lucy's own reaction. Any other woman, knowing that he desired her would have happily laid herself bare for his delectation. But not Lucy. She'd avoided his eye—she'd avoided *him* at all costs. She'd scurried out every night and been there quietly, studiously working every morning. Buttoned up and covered up to within an inch of her life in shapeless boxy suits.

It inflamed him and perplexed him. He'd genuinely never had to deal with this before. But what it was doing was raising the stakes, and raising his blood pressure. He was too proud to force her, even though he knew she wasn't far from tipping over the edge, but damned if he'd do it.

No, she would come to him, just as he'd declared. When she was weak with longing and stir crazy with desire she'd come to him, and this build-up would finally explode in a blaze of mutual satisfaction. He heard the bathroom door click open behind him and shifted in his seat to ease the constriction of his trousers. He picked up some work papers resignedly and it chafed—because he was not a man used to *resigning* himself to things.

For now, though, he'd use work to drown out his clamouring pulse. He would not let her see the roiling waves of frustration that gripped him and tossed him like a tiny boat in a thundering storm. When she came and sat down opposite him, and that sensual womanly smell that was so at odds with her prim appearance teased his nostrils and made his arousal even more acute, he almost groaned.

He looked up for a second. Predictably, she was looking down, immersed in papers. He saw what she'd done to her hair and the firmly reinstated glasses. He felt a surge of adrenalin and thought to himself, *Fine, if that's the way you want it.*

He pulled out his laptop and fired off a curt but informative e-mail to his assistant in Athens, instructing her to have everything ready by the time they landed in two hours. For someone with his wealth and resources, what he'd just asked for shouldn't be hard to pull off, and as he sat back he realised with a jolt that once again he felt more alive than he'd done in months.

The fact that the merger was once again relegated to second place raised just the dimmest clanging bell in his consciousness.

CHAPTER FIVE

A FEW hours later, Lucy sat on the bed of a palatial suite in one of the most expensive hotels in Athens. She'd never seen such opulence and luxury in her life. Everyone here seemed to talk in hushed tones. She'd even found herself almost whispering *thank you* to the concierge who'd shown her to her room.

Her mouth quirked dryly. Needless to say, the manager himself had shown Aristotle to *his* room. She'd seen that they were more or less next door to each other, he in the Royal Suite and she in a smaller adjoining one, although she had no intention of using the interconnecting door that had been pointed out to her. She was already far too close to her boss for comfort.

Feeling antsy, she got up and wandered about the room for a bit, looking out of the window, taking in the view of Syntagma Square and its elegant lines and trees. She hadn't expected Athens to be so…elegant. She'd seen the Acropolis in the distance and felt a lurch of joy; even though she'd travelled extensively due to her peripatetic childhood, she never tired of seeing famous monuments.

Her thoughts went inward. She hadn't failed to notice that the closer they'd got to Athens, the more tense Aristotle had grown—until by the time they'd been walking through the airport, his hand tight on her elbow, he'd been positively radioactive. She knew it had nothing to do with her. She suspected it had something to do with the way that, whenever he had to deal with his stepmother or half-brother, he always seemed to go inwards and become monosyllabic. Clearly there was no love lost between him and his family or his ancestral home, and it made Lucy wonder about that—before she realised what she was doing and put a halt to her wayward thoughts.

She checked her watch. They were due to have informal drinks with Parnassus and his team in one hour and she had to wash and change, but there was still no sign of her luggage. Lucy called down to Reception, and what the girl said made her frown.

'I'm sorry? You say my clothes are here? But I'm still waiting for my case.'

The hotel receptionist's tone was smooth, as if she was used to dealing with recalcitrant hotel guests. 'I think if you check your wardrobe, Miss Proctor you'll find everything hanging up and ready for your use. The chest of drawers is also full.'

Lucy thanked her faintly and put the phone down. She knew that Aristotle's wealth could just about do anything, but surely it couldn't magically conjure up her suitcase, unpack and store all her clothes without her even noticing? With a snaking feeling of *something* slithering down her spine, Lucy threw open the ornate door of the wardrobe in the corner and gasped.

It was full, heaving with a myriad assortment of every piece of clothing any one woman could possibly hope for. Day-wear, casual wear, evening-wear. Lucy flicked past dresses and suits and trousers and shirts and wraps and capes, feeling more and more dizzy as she did so. All sorts of shoes were lined up below the hanging clothes.

She backed away from the wardrobe with something like horror in her chest, and went to open the drawers of the chest beside the wardrobe. She pulled out T-shirts, shorts, casual trousers, capri pants... They all fell from nerveless fingers. There was thousands of euros' worth of clothes in front of her and not one stitch was hers. A deeply scooped-neck T-shirt fell from her hands and she looked at it and shuddered at the thought of how much cleavage *that* would expose. Suddenly realisation struck. *Aristotle*.

Without thinking, galvanised by pure anger, she marched over to that adjoining door between their rooms and yanked it open. To her surprise his own door was already open, leading into a room that made her own opulent one look like a prefab.

He strolled out at that moment from what she presumed must be his bedroom, naked except for a small towel around lean hips. All Lucy could see was a magnificently bronzed muscled chest, a light smattering of dark hair and long, long muscled legs. His hair was wet and slicked back, making him look somehow more approachable, vulnerable.

Seeing him like this completely scrambled her brain and defused her anger.

'I...' She realised she was breathing hard.

He stopped and looked at her enquiringly, and then she watched him lift his wrist to look at the heavy platinum watch.

'A little longer than I thought it might take, but still...not bad.'

It took a few precious seconds for what he said to sink in. He'd planned this. He'd orchestrated this and had been waiting for her to react exactly as she had. Sheer fury and impotence rushed through Lucy in a wave so strong she shook.

'Where is my case, please?'

Aristotle folded his arms and that was worse—because where his shirt might have hidden those biceps, now she could see them in all their olive-skinned, bunched glory. Lord, but he was beautiful, and her body was reacting like the Road Runner, seeing his mate in the distance.

'Your case is somewhere safe. I've taken the liberty of removing the items I think you'll need, like your toiletries. I didn't want to presume to know what products you like to use.'

'Yet you can presume to know what clothes I may like and my size?' Her voice fairly crackled with ice.

His gaze drifted down over her body, and she cursed herself for inciting him. His eyes met hers again and he drawled, 'I think you'll find that everything…fits.'

She cursed him under her breath. She wouldn't be surprised to find them all a size too small, and if they were…

But he wasn't finished. 'I also decided that from what I've seen you're more than capable of choosing your own underwear. You'll find the items I've taken out there, in that bag.'

He gestured to a table nearby, where one of the hotel bags was sitting, a lacy bra strap dangling provocatively from the top. Blind rage and humiliation at the thought he'd handled her intimate clothes, and at remembering that he'd seen her changing, almost made Lucy stumble as she stalked over to get it. But in that instant she vowed she would not react as he was expecting her to. She would not give him the satisfaction.

So she merely walked back to the door, turned and, avoiding his eye, said grimly, 'I'll see you in the lobby in forty-five minutes.'

'I'm looking forward to it, Lucy.'

It took an awful lot of restraint not to slam both interconnecting doors as Lucy went back into her own room, but under a steaming hot shower minutes later she vented her anger with no holds barred.

* * *

Some forty-five minutes later Lucy paced in the lobby and in-effectually tried to pull the dress down again. It felt indecently short, even though it came to just above her knees. She hated the fact that otherwise it fitted like a glove. And she'd never worn shoes with heels so spiky they looked like a lethal weapon, but it had been them or flat shoes, and even *she* had enough fashion pride not to make a complete fool of herself. She also hated the fact that they made her feel some-how…powerful. She couldn't say the word *sexy*. Her brain seized at the mere nebulous thought.

Aristotle watched Lucy from behind a plant for a moment, feeling curiously protective—and something else: surprised at her obvious reluctance to embrace her innate sexiness, es-pecially when she oozed such voluptuous femininity. She'd chosen one of the least revealing dresses, but even that made his blood boil over with lust.

It had a high neck but, unlike her other sack of a dress, this one was cut to define a woman's body, to hug and emphasise its curves. When she turned to the side he had to draw in a breath. Her breasts were so beautifully shaped and enticingly full that he noticed more than one man falter as he saw her.

That galvanised Aristotle to move. Possessiveness was an alien emotion, but it was coursing through him now as he took in the way the dress drew the eye to those stupendously long and slender legs, a discreet slit showcasing their shapeliness. And those shoes…

Lucy turned away abruptly. She'd noticed a man nearly tripping over himself as he'd seen her and she flushed with mortification. He probably thought she was a call girl. She felt like one. This was ridiculous. She was going to demand her own things back—

Suddenly Aristotle was right in front of her and, as was becoming annoyingly familiar, her brain emptied of all rational thought. He was dressed in a black suit, white shirt and royal blue tie. It somehow made his eyes pop out, even though they were a dark slumberous green. But weren't they normally light green? As Lucy was wondering this, as if it had become the most important question in the universe, Aristotle moved so fast that she didn't even notice until he'd whipped her glasses off her face and removed the pins from her hair.

'Hey!' she cried out, too late, only to see him calmly snap her glasses in two and feel the heavy fall of her hair around her shoulders. He took her by the arm and marched her out towards the entrance, handing her broken glasses and hairpins to an unsurprised-looking doorman, who took them obsequiously, clearly not fazed by such behaviour. It made Lucy even madder. Those glasses had been her last bastion of defence and he'd merely ripped it away, like removing a toy from a cranky child.

She barely noticed the pleasantly warm early evening air caressing her skin between the hotel and the luxury car. When they were ensconced in the back, Aristotle curtly ordered the driver to put up the privacy partition, which he duly did. Lucy's mouth was opening and closing ineffectually, steam practically coming out of her ears as Aristotle rounded on her, blocking out any daylight coming through the tinted windows. Absurdly, in that split second Lucy thought how unbearably intimate it seemed to make the space.

'Enough,' he growled out, and before she knew which end was up Aristotle had reached out, hauled her into his chest and his mouth was over hers. He was kissing her as if his life depended on it, one arm like steel across her back, one hand in her hair, clasping her head. There was no hesitation. Lust exploded in a blaze of heat.

All of Lucy's reflex denials melted away in a flame of desire so profound and deep that she couldn't question it. All she knew was that Aristotle's mouth was on hers, his tongue stabbing deep, with ruthless precision, and she was *craving* it. Her breasts were crushed against his chest, her hands trapped against those hard contours, and the beat of his heart was an unsteady tattoo that made her own beat faster.

She forced her hands free to twine them around Aristotle's neck, fingers pushing upwards into the thick, silky hair that brushed his collar. He groaned deep in his throat, their mouths not parting for a moment, lost in a dark, lustrous world of tasting and touching, of sensation heaping on top of sensation so acutely delicious that when Lucy felt herself being lowered back onto the seat behind her, and Aristotle coming over her, she too gave a deep moan of approval.

All she knew was here and now. Sanity had ceased to exist. The outside world? Gone.

This was her world, and this man was the only thing in it. His huge hard body crushed hers to the seat beneath her, but her arms were free and she explored and spread them under his jacket to feel the latent strength of his broad shoulders.

His mouth left hers to blaze a trail of hot kisses along her jaw and down her throat, where he nipped gently and then sucked, making her squirm as an arrow of pure lust shot to her groin, making her wet.

As if he'd read her mind, she felt his hand encircle her ankle and start to travel up her leg. He breathed into her mouth, 'Remember what I said the other day?'

Words couldn't impinge upon her mind in this drenching of desire. Lucy couldn't function. She was finding it hard to open her eyes, finding it hard to breathe as she looked up and drowned in dark green oceans. She didn't recognise the man above her. The expression on his face was so raw and elemental. All she knew was that he looked exactly how she felt. Her breasts were tight and aching, tips chafing against the confining bra and dress. And slowly, so slowly, his hand was climbing with relentless precision, until its heat was wrapped around her upper thigh, where her sheer stockings ended. His fingers spread wide to encompass as much as he could touch. Any second now they'd be on her bare skin. She stopped breathing in earnest.

'Please…' Was that voice hers? Who was she anyway? She was suffering from temporary amnesia. Somewhere distant, where a bell was ringing, she felt something wanting to intrude, but more than that she wanted *this*. It felt so right and so necessary. Too right to question.

'Please… *Ari*…'

With a muffled groan of something that sounded Greek and almost painful, he lowered his head, took her mouth again. Their tongues connected feverishly just as his hand hovered and tantalised at the tender place of her soft inner thigh, on the edge of her silk pants. Lucy tore her mouth away and arched herself towards him, gripping his shoulders. She could feel the heavy stabbing weight of his erection against her leg and she moved experimentally, exulting in his answering growl of unmistakable torture.

And then he was *there*, fingers pushing aside the barrier of her pants to slide into hot slickness, where she ached most. She sucked in a breath, shocked eyes opening wide. She looked up and his fingers began to move, finding the secret spot and pressing it, flicking it. Blood roared into Lucy's head, drowning out everything but the clamour for satisfaction which was coming towards her like the mirage of an oasis in the desert.

And then suddenly, as quickly as this insanity had taken over, it was gone. Aristotle was taking away his hand, moving back, his features harsh and unbearably tight. Cold seeped into Lucy as she realised where she was. She was supine on the back seat of a car, her legs spread, and her boss had just been—

Oh God.

She also realised what Aristotle had realised way before her: they had stopped, obviously at their destination, and the driver was patiently knocking on the privacy window. They hadn't heard him because—

Oh God.

More shame and mortification and self-disgust than she could ever remember feeling coursed through Lucy in a tidal wave of heat so intense she felt feverish. She scrambled to sit up, hands shaking as she pulled her dress down to cover her thighs.

A large brown hand came over hers, and she had to stop herself flinching back.

'OK?'

The huskily asked question surprised her. *It was almost as if he really cared.* But she couldn't look at him, just nodded jerkily, a curtain of hair hiding her face from view. She could give thanks for once that it was down. She didn't think she could ever look at him ever again. In the split seconds they had as they gathered themselves and she heard Aristotle—*Ari*—speak to the driver, Lucy tried to assimilate what had just happened.

The fact that she'd all but drowned in an instantaneous pool of lust in his arms was evident enough. She'd deal with that in a darkened room on her own later. But it was the fact that it had happened without hesitation, with not even a flicker of rejection or desire to draw back. Was it simply because after weeks of denying this to herself, weeks of this desire building and building, the merest touch had sent her up in flames and she'd been unable to draw up even the flimsiest of defences? She'd turned into a complete wanton.

When Aristotle climbed out of the car, and Lucy readied herself to step out too, she realised that any vulnerability she'd felt before had paled into pathetic insignificance. The truth swirled sickeningly in her breast. She truly was her mother's daughter, and that knowledge jeered her for all her efforts to deny it for so long.

There was no going back now, not after that little performance, and she quaked when she saw the huge looming shape materialise on the other side of the door. That everything she feared most lay outside that door right now was obvious, and also the fact that she'd just kissed goodbye to any pretence of a defence she might dream up to excuse her behaviour. The door opened abruptly and Lucy was compelled to step out, taking the hand that was offered and forcing down the frisson of electricity at even that innocuous touch. She felt as though the entire world had changed, and suddenly her place in it.

It was while they were standing alone for a moment, in the luxurious salon of the palatial Parnassus villa on the outskirts of Athens, that Lucy felt Aristotle turn towards her. She closed her eyes momentarily and pleaded silently, *Please don't look at me...please don't say anything.* But since when were her prayers answered? She opened her eyes and gritted her jaw.

Aristotle looked down at Lucy and felt completely out of his depth. He still couldn't quite believe what had happened in the back of his car. He'd never, *ever* been so consumed with lust like that—that he'd laid a woman down in the back seat and all but made love to her there and then. When he thought of it now, of how close he'd been to unzipping his fly—his hand clenched around his drink and he had to force it to unclench.

Lucy hadn't looked at him since she'd stepped out of the car and he couldn't blame her. What was it he'd said? That he wouldn't be a lecherous boss? And then within seconds of getting into an enclosed space... But she'd been so responsive, dammit. Like his most potent dream, his hottest fantasy. She'd been hot, willing, passionate...*wet* for him. His body tightened again. She'd shown him the woman she was hiding under all that primness.

It was hard to equate the woman who'd paled at seeing her bra strap hanging out of a bag earlier to the woman who'd almost come apart in his arms less than a couple of hours ago.

'Lucy?'

He could see her grit her jaw, and it was only then that he noticed the faint pink mark on her neck. Shock coursed through him—and self-disgust. He'd given her a love bite? The last time he'd given a woman a love bite it had been a *girl*, and in a boarding school in England, probably at the age of thirteen. All of a sudden Aristotle felt anger for what this woman was reducing him to.

He took her arm and tried to ignore the way her skin felt, tried to ignore the way he wanted to caress it, tried to ignore the way she looked almost green.

'Lucy, look at me.'

With the utmost reluctance Lucy turned her head and looked up, willing her reaction far down. She even pasted a smile on her face. 'Yes?'

Aristotle looked angry. 'Lucy…' He sighed with exasperation and ran his other hand through his hair, leaving it to flop back in such sexy disarray that Lucy felt her knees tremble.

'I had no intention of kissing you like that, and I'm sorry. It shouldn't have happened—'

'No, it shouldn't.'

His eyes narrowed dangerously. He turned so that the room was blocked out and it was just the two of them facing each other.

'That's not what I meant. I was going to say it shouldn't have happened *like that*.'

'Well, it shouldn't have happened at all.'

Aristotle's brow went up. Lucy hated that brow.

'Are you going to try and tell me that you didn't like it? Or that I was mauling you again? What was it you called me? *Ari*?'

'Stop it,' Lucy hissed, a crimson tide washing into her face when she remembered that passionate entreaty, how easily it had fallen from her lips. 'Of course I'm not going to say…that. But it shouldn't have happened, and it's not going to happen again.'

Aristotle moved closer, and Lucy realised that she couldn't move back as there was a plant behind her. His heat and that innately musky scent came and wrapped itself around her, binding her into the memory of what had happened, making longing rush through her. And she hated it.

Aristotle's face was a harsh mask of self-recrimination as he said, 'It *will* be happening again, Lucy—just not in the back seat of a car. Somewhere infinitely more comfortable, where we won't be constricted by space and hampered by clothes.'

Just then someone approached, and Aristotle smoothly turned to deal with the newcomer, stunning Lucy with his ability to morph from intensely demanding alpha male to urbane businessman. And for the rest of the evening, as she accompanied him around the room, meeting and greeting the people involved in the Parnassus side of the merger, she could almost be forgiven for thinking she'd imagined the whole thing.

While they were in Athens Lucy was to be Aristotle's executive assistant. She'd met Martha, his Greek PA, a pleasant older lady who she'd spoken to on the phone before. She met them at the hotel earlier. *She* was going to deal with the day-to-day office stuff. Martha wasn't aware of the merger. In fact none of his family seemed to be—something which had perplexed Lucy.

Mr Parnassus approached them now, distracting her from her thoughts. He and Aristotle had already gone to his study for a private meeting as soon as they'd arrived. Now this old and stooped man, who walked with a cane, looked Lucy up and down with a wink. They'd been introduced earlier.

He said to Aristotle, 'Well, Ari, do you think we can trust her?'

Aristotle's voice was deep and authoritative. 'Absolutely. She's been with my firm for over two years now.'

As they continued to converse, Lucy decided that she liked Parnassus. He had a friendly twinkle in his eye. Suddenly he declared that Aristotle should go and mingle so that he could 'take this beautiful young woman outside for a turn around the patio'.

At a pointed look from her boss that Lucy couldn't really fathom, she gave her arm to Parnassus and led the way outside. It was night and the sky was clear, stars twinkling over a commanding view down into Athens. Momentarily relieved to be out of Aristotle's disturbing orbit, Lucy breathed in. 'It's so beautiful here. You have a lovely home, Mr Parnassus.'

'Please, call me Georgios.'

Lucy smiled. 'Very well. Georgios.'

He looked at her with shrewd eyes. 'He must trust you very much. This merger is very important. Not even his own family know about it.'

Lucy's belly clenched painfully. It wasn't so much about trust as necessity and desire, but of course she couldn't explain that. She frowned slightly. 'I'm aware of that.' She didn't want to say more. She didn't know Aristotle's reasons for not divulging this to his family, and she knew the only reason they were here in Athens was because Parnassus had requested it.

'He's driven.'

Lucy was lost in her thoughts for a moment. She almost didn't hear what the man said. But he was continuing, looking down at the view laid out before them.

'He reminds me of myself when I was his age.' Parnassus

smiled, but it seemed sad. 'He reminds me of my own son. In exile. Driven to succeed at all costs. And for what?'

Lucy was nonplussed. Parnassus caught her look and chuckled. 'I'm sorry—you don't want to hear an old man's ramblings. We should go back inside.'

She put out a hand. 'Oh, not at all... I just... I don't know Ar—' She blushed. 'That is, I don't know Mr Levakis all that well.'

Parnassus stalled and looked at her closely. He gestured with an arm to encompass the view and the villa. 'See all this?'

Lucy nodded and sat back against the balustrade, captivated by this wizened man, by his deeply ingrained accent which he obviously hadn't lost despite living in the US for decades.

'It's taken me years to build it up. My family left this country in shame, and all I've ever wanted was to come back in a blaze of glory.'

Lucy frowned. 'But...that's what you're doing with this merger, isn't it?'

He shrugged one bony shoulder. '*Ack*. In some ways. It's not how I imagined it, even though I'll get what *I* want for my children, whether they want it or not: re-introduction and acceptance into Athens society. But the ultimate glory will belong to that man in there, and he's welcome to it.'

They both looked to where Aristotle stood, surrounded by a fawning crowd. Lucy shivered slightly despite the treacherous heat curling down low in her abdomen. He reminded her of a lone wolf. Head and shoulders above everyone else, supremely confident, supremely sexy and yet...*alone*. She hadn't really thought of him like that before, and didn't like the tender feelings it aroused.

At that moment a very glamorous-looking middle-aged woman came out to the terrace. Parnassus introduced her as his wife, bade Lucy goodnight and went back inside. Lucy turned to face the view again, her mind full of questions. She wrapped her arms around herself, feeling a sudden cool breeze. What did Parnassus mean about Aristotle? Did he somehow see him heading for an empty life, driven by a need to succeed? Clearly he wasn't far wrong. Aristotle had said himself that this merger was the most important thing, and yet—

She jumped when she felt a warm blanket of heat settle around her shoulders and heard a deep, 'We should get going. We've got a busy day tomorrow.'

His jacket was warm with his body heat and scent. It enveloped Lucy, making her sway a little as they went back in. She didn't say a word. Every nerve was twanging at the thought of sharing a car with him again, and her head was bursting with all the enigmatic questions Parnassus had posed.

But she needn't have worried. Aristotle couldn't have made it clearer he had no intention of touching her. Lucy sat in her corner and watched as they were driven down the hill towards the city centre. Feeling somehow compelled, she turned to face Aristotle and asked, 'Don't you have a family home here?'

She sensed him tensing, but he just said, without looking at her, 'Yes, it was my father's home, but I prefer to stay in a hotel.'

And then, before Lucy could halt her runaway mouth, she heard herself asking, 'Why don't your family know about the merger?'

His head whipped around so fast that she nearly flinched back. The lines in his face were stark. 'What makes you ask that?' The thread of warning was explicit.

Lucy shrugged. 'I just…wondered.'

'None of them are aware,' hc said curtly. 'And I've already told you they must not know. As far as they're concerned I'm here for three weeks to check up on the Athens side of the business.'

Lucy's jaw clenched. 'I know all that, and of course I won't be telling them anything. I'm well aware of the terms of my *contract*.'

She turned her head away, stunned to feel a welling of emotion and discover that she had sudden tears stinging the backs of her eyes. What on earth was *that* about?

When she felt her hand being taken by a much larger, warmer one, her heart tripped. She looked around warily. She couldn't really see Aristotle's face in the dark gloom.

He sounded weary all of a sudden. 'Look, it's complicated, OK? It's family stuff between them and me and they just don't need to know. It's for security reasons…'

'That's all you had to say.' Lucy took her hand from his and took off his jacket, handing it back to him. 'I'm warm enough now, thanks.'

Boss/assistant. The lines of demarcation were unmistakable. Aristotle cursed himself again for having lost control earlier. In all honesty the depth of that desire still shook him up. He took the jacket and watched as she turned her head to look out of the window again. The curve of her cheekbone, the fall of her hair was an enticing temptation to turn her face back, seek out those warm lips, sink into her yielding soft body again.

He swore under his breath. He'd vowed he wouldn't take her like some randy over-sexed teenager, but here he was mentally stripping her, moments away from trying to seduce her all over again. He sat rigid in his seat the whole way back to the hotel. *Never* had a woman caused him this much frustration.

When they got back to the hotel Lucy skittered away from him like a scared foal. He let her go, bidding her goodnight, then went into the bar and ordered himself a shot of whisky. It was going to be a long three weeks.

* * *

Towards the end of that first week, Lucy half heard a question from Aristotle as they sat in his office in the centre of Athens. In essence they were conducting separate lives: presenting a benign face to his Athens-based company, and conducting top secret meetings with Parnassus at the same time. The meetings with Parnassus' side were complicated and technical, calling on all of Lucy's skills and much of the small amount of legal training she'd done.

She'd met his stepmother Helen and half-brother Anatolios, at a general board meeting that morning. The step-mother was tall and thin and cold, effortlessly supercilious. His half-brother was nothing like Aristotle. He was blond, shorter and had a spoilt, weak-looking face. It hadn't taken Lucy much to deduce that his brother had a serious jealousy complex as he'd frowned sulkily throughout the meeting, clearly hating having Aristotle back to remind everyone who the *real* boss was. After meeting them, she didn't entirely blame Aristotle for wanting to keep his distance.

'...to put in an appearance at the charity ball tonight.'

Lucy realised she was being spoken to and looked up. 'I'm sorry...?'

Her voice drifted away as she was caught by the gleam in Aristotle's eyes. They were sitting close together, side by side at a table, with papers strewn everywhere. For the whole week, ever since the night they'd arrived and that earth-shattering moment in the car, she'd been rigid with tension, happily throwing herself into work to try and escape from dealing with...*this*.

But it hummed around them now, this awareness. She'd been so careful not to let it catch her unawares, but she had failed in this instance. And in all honesty she knew that it was largely to do with Aristotle's own restraint. He'd been cool and solicitous all week. Not a hint of what had happened in his behaviour. At first it had thrown her, she'd been absurdly suspicious, but now… She realised it had been there all along. She knew it and he knew it, and much to her utter shame a flutter of dark excitement erupted deep in her belly.

She tried to ignore it. 'I'm sorry—what did you say?'

Aristotle looked at her and stifled a groan. Her eyes were huge pools of swirling grey, like a stormy ocean, with lashes so long and dark he could already imagine them fluttering against his cheek. *How* he'd managed not to touch her all week he couldn't really fathom. It had taken super-human restraint, but he'd been determined to prove to himself that she didn't exert that much control over him. Except it had been an exercise in failure, because she did. His mind had constantly been taken from business.

It didn't help that because of the wardrobe he'd provided, which was perfectly respectable, she was unwittingly displaying more of her luscious body. He knew she was deliberately choosing the most *un*revealing clothes, but conversely they were making him want to unwrap her like a delicious parcel.

At the board meeting earlier, when he'd seen his own half-brother's eyes riveted to Lucy's cleavage, he'd wanted to reach across the table and punch him in the face. Being driven to violence by a woman was a very novel experience, and he had to put it down to sexual frustration.

He cleared his throat and dragged his eyes back up, vowing silently to himself that he'd have her in his bed within twenty-four hours. He couldn't take much more of this.

'The charity ball tonight. Everyone will be there—including Parnassus. Needless to say it'll be seen entirely as a coincidence that we're there too. When we meet any of his people we'll affect no knowledge of having met before.'

Lucy had seen the extent of the security detail that both Aristotle and Parnassus commanded, so there had been no chance of a leak. Again the size and importance of what they were working on stunned her.

She asked abruptly, '*Why* is it so important that nobody knows of this, exactly?'

Aristotle's mouth thinned. 'Because our two companies merging will put a lot of noses out of joint. We'll effectively be blowing any competition out of the water; the only companies who will remain safe are the ones who are huge enough to withstand the pressure—people like Kouros Shipping, for instance.'

Lucy nodded, she'd heard of Alexandros Kouros. 'But…your family?'

His eyes flashed at her persistence, but he answered tightly, 'My stepmother and brother would oppose this absolutely. Helen would see it as a dilution of my father's name and a threat to her security. If my brother had even an inkling of this happening he'd do his best to derail it just to get at me. That's why we have to be vigilant. And they'll be at the ball tonight too.' His mouth twisted. 'Although I wouldn't worry about *him* too much—no doubt he'll be more concerned about scoring the best drugs and the best women.'

Lucy hid her shock at this evidence of little love lost. She quashed her immediate questions. She had no desire to know about Aristotle's family history. None at all.

CHAPTER SIX

THAT evening, after they'd eaten a sumptuous dinner, Lucy found herself separated from Aristotle. She was feeling almost relaxed, which she knew had something to do with the fact that she'd been seated apart from him, even though she'd felt the weight of his gaze from across the table, periodically.

She'd been seated next to Kallie Kouros, the wife of Alexandros Kouros, who'd proved to be down to earth and utterly charming, giving Lucy hilarious tidbits of information about Athenian society. When her gorgeous husband had come to whisk her away they'd looked so in love, and he'd been so innately protective, it had made a very secret part of Lucy ache... It surprised her, as she'd never found herself envious of happy couples before.

Lucy craned her neck to try and find Aristotle, not even sure why she felt compelled to do so when he was clearly only too happy to leave her to her own devices. Finally she saw him across the room, with his head bent towards a very blonde and very beautiful woman. She saw him smile and it impacted her deeply. He'd never smiled at *her* like that. *Yes, he did*, reminded a little voice. *That night outside your apartment.*

Immediately she could feel her blood cooling, the colour draining from her face. A strange falling feeling made her feel shaky all of a sudden. On a complete reflex, to deny her reaction and the fact that it might possibly be stemming from feeling *jealous*, she whirled around and made blindly for the ladies room.

After collecting herself she went to the sink and splashed some cold water on her face. When she stood up again she nearly jumped out of her skin to see Helen Levakis, Aristotle's stepmother standing beside her, reapplying her blood-red lipstick.

She looked at Lucy and said, 'Lizzie, wasn't it?'

Lucy shook her head, fascinated by this woman's brittle shell. 'Lucy.'

The woman smiled insincerely. 'My apologies. Ari seems to have a new assistant every time he comes home.'

Lucy washed her hands briskly. 'It's no problem.'

Helen Levakis turned and rested back against the ledge. 'You're sleeping with him, aren't you? I saw that little look outside, when you saw him with another woman.'

Lucy tried and knew she was probably failing to keep the shock from her face. This woman had stuck a knife right into the tender heart of her, and to realise that was huge.

She found her voice. 'Excuse me, but I really don't think it's any of your—'

'You're right,' the woman dismissed cuttingly. 'However, I thought I'd do you a favour. Ari may *sleep* with a woman like you, but he'll never marry a woman like you. That's more than likely why he's home. He'll be looking for a suitable bride soon. A man like him? He'll want to have an heir to secure his inheritance. He'll do anything to stop his brother getting what's rightfully his.'

Lucy watched the tall thin woman disappear back out into the bustling throng with a last glacial glance. She turned to face the mirror, realised that she was holding her breath and let it out in a big whoosh. What on earth had precipitated that? And what did she mean about his brother? And was Ari really looking for a suitable bride as well as the merger? And was she really that transparent?

Lucy forced herself to stand tall and looked at herself critically. She'd chosen one of the less revealing dresses, but still she wanted to yank it up and pull it down. One-shouldered, silk, it cut across her bosom far too low for her liking, and showed a veritable acreage of pale skin, which she was very conscious of in this milieu of much skinnier, more sun-kissed people.

The dark grey seemed to make her eyes stand out too large in her face, and her hectic flush had nothing to do with make-up and everything to do with embarrassment that everyone in the room must have seen her mooning after her boss. Well, it ended here. For the next two weeks it was work only. She'd keep Aristotle at arm's length however she could. A dart of doubt struck her. How did she know he hadn't already transferred his affections to that blonde? Perhaps he'd finally grown weary of chasing his too tall and too buxom secretary?

Choking back a frustrated cry at her own awful weakness and feeling so vulnerable, she left the bathroom—every intention of going back to the hotel. She got out to the lobby and retrieved her coat. She'd just leave a note for—

'Where have you been?'

A hard hand whirled her around so fast she lost her balance and ended up plastered against Aristotle's chest, looking up, slightly winded. When she realised what she was doing she scrambled back, inarticulate anger rushing through her. 'I'm going back to the hotel. I'm tired.'

'Well, I'm not—and we're not finished here.'

'It's a social event. Surely you don't need me to work.'

'I…' Ari faltered. He'd been about to say, *I do need you.* But she was right. It wasn't for work, and if it wasn't for work then what was it? Had he got so used to her calm, insightful presence? Had he really missed her throughout dinner?

He made the only decision he could. 'Fine, then I'll escort you back.'

A huge neon danger sign flashed over Lucy's head. 'No!' She tempered her response. 'I mean—you stay. I don't want to drag you away…' *From that blonde you were obviously enjoying so much.*

But in his usual arrogant way he'd already taken her arm and was leading her outside, where as if by magic his car drew up in front of them.

She tried again in the car. 'Really, you should stay.'

He quirked a small hard smile, leaning back easily, studying her. 'Oh, really? Should I?'

Lucy's hands twisted in her lap. She felt something intangible shift between them. The energy was palpable. 'Yes…' Why did her voice sound breathy all of a sudden? 'Yes,' she said again, stronger. 'You should. You obviously have…people to talk to.'

Aristotle grimaced when he recalled trying to evade the clutches of Pia Kyriapoulos just now. A very beautiful and very wealthy divorcee, she'd made it quite clear what he could expect if he wanted to indulge in an affair while in Athens. Before, he might have been tempted—she was offering just what he liked, no-strings sex—but now…the only woman he wanted was sitting just a few inches away from him, and he couldn't contemplate sex with anyone else.

'You're wrong, Lucy,' he drawled in deep honeyed tones. 'There's no one I want to talk to, and I am only too happy to escort you back.'

Lucy stifled a retort and looked out of the window, a mixture of dread and excitement licking through her when she remembered the last time he'd insisted on taking her home.

Far too soon they were pulling up outside their hotel. Lucy scrambled inelegantly from the car before her door could be opened. But of course her attempts were futile. Aristotle caught up with her easily and took her arm again, leading them over to the gleaming lifts.

Once inside, standing apart from him, Lucy looked up resolutely. She nearly collapsed when she heard Aristotle say innocuously, 'Do you remember the first time we met in a lift?'

Shocked and aghast, she looked at him—and realised too late that it was a mistake. 'The first time we…?'

'Met in a lift,' he said easily, turning to look up at the display. 'Funnily enough, the day you walked into my office to interview for the job I remembered it.' He looked back down at her. 'In vivid detail.'

Lucy was barely aware that she was still standing. She wanted to put out a hand to hold onto something, but the only solid thing was *him*. She prayed she wouldn't collapse.

She shook her head. 'No,' she croaked…and then knew she couldn't lie. 'That is…yes. I remember you using the staff lift, but I don't remember much else.'

Her heart was thumping as all she could remember right then was how hard his body had felt underneath hers. A lot like it had felt *over* hers the other day in the car.

The lift doors opened and Lucy almost fell out. Aristotle walked alongside her easily. Her legs were trembling. As she tried and failed to stick her keycard in her door she felt it taken out of her hand imperiously, and watched helplessly when he effortlessly opened the door.

When she stepped in he said quietly, 'Who knew you were such a consummate liar, Lucy Proctor?'

She turned around, affronted. 'What's that supposed to mean?' She saw that he'd neatly stepped into the room too, and when the door closed behind him her heart seemed to spasm in her chest. 'And what do you think you're doing in here?'

'Proving what a liar you are, Lucy Proctor.'

And then he reached out, two big hands encompassing her waist, and pulled her inexorably towards him, towards that searing heat. Lucy, gripped by an awful feeling of inevitability, stumbled right into his chest.

'This is much better,' Aristotle growled as she fell against him, and he lifted his hands to cup her face and thread fingers through her hair. 'Now I have you exactly where I want you.'

Lucy couldn't help a groan of reluctant supplication when he bent his head and took her mouth. It felt as if he'd injected some kind of life force into her body. Every nerve came tinglingly alive, her heart-rate sped up, her skin seemed to glow...and down below, between her legs, she could already feel her traitorous body responding hotly, wetly.

His tongue swirled, sought hers, sucked it deep into his mouth. She felt fireworks explode in her head. Then he was nipping gently at her lower lip and sucking it, exploring the gap in her teeth and saying throatily, 'Bite me...'

A feeling of exultation took her over. She felt him push her coat off her shoulders to the floor and hardly noticed. Experimentally, shyly, she bit down on his sensual lower lip, feeling its cushiony springiness, soothing with her tongue where she'd bitten.

He growled something indecipherable, and then she felt him searching for and undoing the zip at the side of her dress, pulling it aside so that one lace covered breast was bared. He lifted a hand and cupped its weight. Lucy bit her lip. She felt heavy, aching with a pooling of desire, and it was such an alien feeling it held her in its grip.

One of his big hands reached down and cupped her round buttocks, drawing her up and into him, where she could feel his arousal digging into soft flesh. She felt more liquid heat and instinctively closed her legs against it.

He was palming her breast, a thumb hovering teasingly

over the puckered tip, Tension mounted until Lucy wanted to scream, and finally he lowered his head. Her own fell back when she felt that tight, aching lace-covered tip being drawn into the hot, sucking spiral of intense desire that was his mouth.

His hand gripped her buttock and she strained upwards, urging him to suck harder, her hips moving sinuously against his. She was seeking for a pinnacle that she'd never experienced before, but she knew it was there somewhere.

Something made Lucy open her eyes, and she drew in a shocked breath when she saw their reflections in the mirror across the room, highlighted by the one dim lamp in the corner. They must have moved from the door somehow, although Lucy knew that an earthquake might have happened and she wouldn't have noticed. The image shocked her to the core. It was so explicit…and so like something she'd witnessed as a child, when she'd walked in on her mother unannounced one day.

Sanity and reality didn't trickle back—they exploded in her face. In a second she'd pushed Aristotle away and was pulling up her dress to cover her heaving breasts. She shook violently.

'Get out of here—*now*.'

She spied something from the corner of her eye and moved, grabbing the hotel robe from the end of her bed and pulling it on, wrapping it tightly around her, belting it firmly. She went and stood near the window, her brain hurting and her body throbbing with unfulfilled desire.

'*Please* just get out.'

'No, Lucy, I won't.' Aristotle's voice was unbearably harsh.

She could only imagine how angry he must be with her. She knew what men called women who—

'Look, I'm sorry. I should never have let that happen—it's entirely my fault.'

'You didn't *let* it happen, Lucy. You weren't helpless. You wanted it as much as I did.'

She shook her head dumbly and felt tears threaten.

Aristotle stepped forward then, and stopped a few feet away. His face looked as if it was carved from stone and Lucy quaked inwardly. She wanted to say sorry again, but didn't. His bow-tie was askew, his hair ruffled. Had she done that?

He frowned, as if trying to understand. 'Lucy, did someone do something to you? Did someone hurt you?'

She shook her head quickly. 'No…nothing like that.'

He shook his head. 'Well, if it's not that…what is it?'

She felt like crying in earnest now. How could she get into her tangled emotional history? Into how threatened she felt by the way he made her feel?

'I just…I don't want this. I don't want to *feel* this way.' It was the closest she could come to an admission.

Aristotle was unsympathetic. 'Well, tough—because you do and I do. It's called chemistry and it's unavoidable.'

'What if I leave?' Lucy asked hopefully.

He shook his head. 'We've been through this. You're not going anywhere.'

Her shoulders slumped, and she missed the flash of something that crossed Aristotle's face.

'Look,' Lucy began awkwardly, 'I'm not experienced— I'm not like the women you go for. I won't know how to…'

'You already do, sweetheart, without even trying.'

She looked up. It seemed important to say it. 'I'm not a virgin…I've had sex before.' *Once.* 'But I didn't feel anything. So I know that…it won't do anything for me.'

He came close and tipped her chin up. Lucy tried to avoid his eye but it was impossible.

'Are you seriously trying to tell me that you think you won't enjoy having sex?'

She shrugged, feeling very silly.

'Lucy, in case you haven't noticed, you're a sensualist. That's the only word I can find to describe you. Even though you seem determined to deny it, and I've no idea why that is. Don't you know why you have a taste for exotic underwear?'

'It's because…' Lucy stopped, remembering all those shopping trips with her mother—how she'd had it drummed into her how important it was to buy decent underclothes. But of course other teenage girls hadn't had the privilege of shopping with the scandalous Maxine Malbec.

'It's because I developed too early. I'm too…' her face burnt and she was glad of the dim light '…big. To get the right sizes you have to pay more…'

His hand still gripped her chin. 'Lucy, there's a whole nation of women out there bigger than you who wear woefully fitting underwear. Can't you just admit that you're drawn to it? To the feel of it against your skin? How it fits and makes you look—'

She tore his hand away and stepped back further. 'No.' But she knew his words had made an impact. *Did* she instinctively like it? *Was* she a sensualist, despite everything—just like her mother? Well, she'd proven spectacularly that in all other respects their shared genes certainly seemed to be showing themselves.

'No. Look…I have my reasons for not wanting this. I just…want you to respect that.'

Ari fought the most intense battle of his life as he looked at her downbent head and the tightly drawn belt on the robe. His body burned and ached. He felt hard from tip to toe and couldn't believe she was denying them this.

But he found some strength from somewhere. He stepped close again and saw the way Lucy's body tensed even more. In that instant something inside him melted. He wanted this woman with a passion he'd never known before, but he didn't want to force her. He felt an uncomfortable level of concern grip him as he tipped her chin up to see her face. She avoided his eyes. He felt her grit her jaw against his hand and his stomach clenched. He rubbed his thumb back and forth over silky smooth skin. The bones felt unbelievably delicate. Her jaw finally relaxed, and something akin to triumph moved through him.

Suddenly the urge to take Lucy to bed was superseded by his wanting to reassure her. He had the insane impulse to pull her close and tell her everything was going to be OK. Something deeply ingrained within him kept him from making the move, but it made his voice husky.

'I'm going to leave, but I want you to think about this, Lucy. What's between us is more than a banal attraction that happens every day of the week. This is…' His own words surprised him, and so did the emotion he could feel behind them, but he told himself it was just because he wanted her so badly. ' This is something much stronger. I don't know what demons you're fighting, and I can't fight them for you. Only you can do that. I'm going to leave the interconnecting door to my room open. I'd like you to use it, Lucy…I want to explore what this is with you…'

His mouth twisted. 'I've no doubt it'll burn itself out, but it's not going to go away until we do explore it. It's just going to get stronger. It's up to you. If you're strong enough to resist this then by God I hope you have enough strength for the both of us.'

Lucy's breath had stalled, and because it was hard not to she found herself staring directly into his eyes. What she saw there made her heart twist. It wasn't the heated intensity she'd expected—well, *it was*—but it didn't make her feel threatened. It made her feel quivery and achy, as if she wanted to throw caution to the wind and say *yes*.

For a long moment they stood like that, his words hanging

heavy in the air, and all Lucy's nerves seemed to centre on the hand which felt so warm and oddly reassuring on her jaw. But then Aristotle was taking that hand away and stepping back. He turned and walked to the door. In a second he was gone, and the room felt huge and cavernously empty. Bereft. In mere seconds she heard him opening the interconnecting door on his side and flinched slightly at the sound.

She went and sat heavily on the bed, feeling sick in her belly, his words swirling in her head. Was he right? Would this only get stronger? The ripples of sensation still pouring through her body mocked her. Who was she kidding? She'd fooled herself that it had receded this week, but he was right—especially if her reaction just now was anything to go by.

She'd also, she had to acknowledge, fooled herself into thinking she was frigid. Right now she felt like the least frigid person on the planet. She had to recognise that in losing her virginity she'd subconsciously gone out and deliberately chosen someone she didn't feel attracted to—as if to try and convince herself that she wasn't like her mother, that she wouldn't spend her life craving sex.

She frowned at that. It sounded wrong as she thought it now. She'd always believed her mother to have craved sex…but in actual fact it had been the men, their power and attention. She'd sought validation from *that*. When Lucy really thought about it, her mother had always been quite cool and clinical about sex. She'd never become so passionate about a man that she'd lost sight of practicalities.

The way Lucy felt about Aristotle right now had nothing to do with being cool and clinical. He could be the hotel doorman and he'd still have this effect on her. While Lucy knew for a fact that her mother would never in a million years have spared a mere doorman a second glance.

Seeing herself and Ari reflected in the mirror, the look on her face—it *hadn't* been the same as her mother's that day.

She'd never seen her mother look like that. So…desirous, so caught up in the moment.

The revelation stunned her now. Because of her mother's profession, and how overtly sexual it had been, she'd always assumed that Maxine's myriad liaisons had been all about sex. But they hadn't. They'd been about money and power and her mother's self-esteem. Not sex. That had merely been a tool she'd used. Lucy had *known* this, but it had taken the awakening of her own desire to really *see* it for the first time.

One of Lucy's biggest fears had to do with losing her independence by depending on men as her mother had done. But wasn't this a totally different situation? She was working; she already had a job. She wasn't hoping to get anything out of Aristotle—certainly not money or gifts. And he seemed to be as surprised by this flaring of attraction as she was. She had no doubt that if he had a choice he'd prefer this to be happening with someone in his own social group.

So didn't it stand to reason that once this thing had *burnt out*, as he'd said, things would get back to normal? Although Lucy had to concede she didn't know what it would mean to get back to *normal* in the office after something like this…her mind skittered weakly away from that.

She was pacing now, the thought of sleep impossible to consider. She bit at her nail, a tight feeling growing in her belly. For the first time in her life the fears she'd carried for so long about turning into her mother and all that meant seemed flimsy—they didn't hold water any more. *She was different.* The warm feeling of reassurance she'd imagined she'd felt just now surged back even stronger. And it scared her slightly, as she'd never in a million years have said that Ari was a *reassuring* type of man.

She stopped pacing. What if she could do this? Instead of running away, why not face this and vanquish the demons that had been plaguing her? Already she felt different; she had to admit she'd enjoyed the less restrictive wardrobe, and even though her reflex was still to cover up it was diminishing. She'd caught some of the men looking at her earlier in the ballroom, and instead of wanting to hide away she'd found herself straightening up, feeling a very fledgling sense of confidence trickling through her.

Had Aristotle helped her come to this? It didn't feel like the diminishing needy power that she'd seen her mother crave. It felt like an innately feminine power, pure and strong.

She thought about it again, tested the words: what if she did this? Just went over there to that door, opened it and walked through.

Before she knew her legs had even carried her Lucy stood at the door, breathing short shallow breaths, her heart thumping. She'd once read a book: *Feel the Fear and Do it Anyway*. Was she brave enough? To step across the line?

As if in answer to her own question, an intense yearning spread through her. She wanted this—wanted this man and what he promised more than she wanted to look at all the reasons for not doing it. He was right. The thought of repressing this desire was…inconceivable.

With a shaking hand she touched the doorknob, took a breath and turned it. She shut her eyes as the door opened silently. A lurid mental image of Aristotle lounging back against black silk sheets, hands behind his head with a mocking smile, nearly made her slam it shut. But she resisted the impulse and opened her eyes.

It took a second for Lucy's eyes to adjust, and the scene greeting her was as erotically charged as she could have imagined and yet surprisingly benign. Through the open bedroom door, across the wide expanse of opulent sitting room, Lucy could see the reflected figure of a sleeping Aristotle in his bed in a slightly open mirrored wardrobe door.

Far from black silk, the sheets he lay on were white, like

hers. He'd thrown off the main covers and lay now, half propped up, with just a sheet hitched up to his waist. She'd seen his naked torso the other day, but now she looked her fill. It was long and lean and bronzed and hard, and exquisitely muscled. More superlatives filled her head but she couldn't articulate them. He was simply the most devastating specimen of a man she'd ever seen—not that she'd seen many, she had to acknowledge wryly, but she felt fairly sure that Aristotle could take his place among some of the most beautiful men on the planet.

Unruly inky black hair flopped with incongruous youthfulness onto his forehead, making him look much less like the feared CEO of Levakis Enterprises and instead like someone altogether more vulnerable and human.

Lucy's breath snagged when her eyes rested on those lean hips and then moved down lower, to where the strategically placed sheet was tented slightly over his lap. Hot colour poured into her cheeks at the intense and immediate reaction to even such subtle provocation.

A sound made her eyes dart up, and suddenly the sleeping god of perfection was no more—he was awake, light green eyes darkening even as she looked at him. Lucy belatedly realised that, as if in a dream, she'd walked right into his room and was now standing at the foot of his bed, the dim light of one lamp imbuing everything with innate intimacy.

Her hands gripped the sides of her robes together, knuckles showing white. Reality slammed into her, and she suddenly wondered if she'd suffered some kind of paralysis as she couldn't seem to move.

'I...'

Aristotle was completely still, awake and watchful now.

'You...?'

The sound of his voice resonated deep within her.

'I...I don't think... That is...perhaps I should—'

'Come here.'

The words were uttered with deep implacability, and Lucy's legs felt shaky. She'd come too far to go back now, so she moved forward jerkily, around the bed, until she was standing just a few feet away, eyes glued to his, mesmerised.

He lifted a hand and gestured. 'Come closer.'

Lucy looked desperately for any sign that he mightn't be as *über*-cool as he looked. And at the last second, just when she was contemplating running while she still could, she saw it: the light sheen of sweat beading his brow and the pulse beating fast at the base of his neck.

But, even so, it was as if the old, safe Lucy was calling her back through the doors, willing her to slam them shut between her and this man and this craving, aching need within her. She even turned and looked, as if to judge the distance.

Immediately her hand was taken in a ring of heat. Lucy looked down to see her wrist dwarfed by his bronzed hand. She looked at him, and gulped.

'Lucy, are you sure you want this? Because if you stay there's no going back.'

And in that instant Lucy mentally shut the doors behind her. She didn't want to go back. She wanted to go forward and free herself of this unwanted baggage she'd been carrying.

She shook her head and felt her hair slip around her shoulders. 'I'm not going.'

He pulled her irrevocably towards him, and then she was there, legs leaning weakly against his bed, His eyes never left hers as he brought her wrist to his mouth and pressed a kiss against the pulse, his tongue flicking out. She gasped and felt as if he'd branded her, even with that small move.

And then he let her hand go and leant on one elbow. 'Take off your clothes.'

When he said the words, Lucy felt only an intense explosion of heat in her pelvis. She was far beyond disgust or shock. Without breaking eye contact she undid her thick robe and let it drop to the floor. She still wore the dress, which gaped open, and her shoes. She stepped out of the shoes and bent to put them neatly under the chair. Then she stood and looked at Aristotle again.

He had made no move, but his eyes had turned so dark with lust that the green looked almost black. His gaze burnt into her.

With a tremor in her hands she pulled the zip down all the way, and then slowly peeled the dress off her shoulder and down, baring breasts only just confined by a strapless lace bra. Her awful self-consciousness seemed to have faded away to another place. Another person.

Hands on her hips, Lucy wriggled slightly to ease the dress down and over her womanly shape. The veritable waves of heat coming from Aristotle as his eyes followed the path of her dress nearly had Lucy melting on the spot. The heavy silk pooled at her feet, and she stepped out with an innate grace she was entirely unaware of.

Seeing a heavily brocaded chair beside the bed, Lucy lifted one leg to rest her foot there and started to peel one stocking down, only belatedly becoming aware of the eroticism of her pose. She sensed it in the way Ari had stilled even more, felt it in the intensity of his gaze on her, and for the first time in her life, found herself glorying in her innate femininity.

Aristotle knew that the only thing keeping him from jumping out of the bed and burying his aching hardness into her as she bent like that over the chair was the knowledge that, given one touch of her skin, he'd lose all control. When he'd seen her standing at the foot of the bed like a vision, his feeling of pure desire twinned with what had felt suspiciously like joy had made him act gruffer than he would have liked. He gripped the sheets tight in both hands now. It felt hard to breathe. The fact that he also felt more out of control than he'd ever felt with another woman was uncomfortable. Finesse in this kind of situation was a distant memory.

A curtain of dark hair swung forward, restricting his view of the bountiful breasts threatening to spill from that completely inadequate bra, and instinctively he leant forward and brushed it back over one pale shoulder. She turned her head and looked at him, her lower lip caught by her teeth, sending a shudder of pure arousal through his body, tightening the erotic notch on his flimsy control.

She put down that leg and lifted the other, repeated the exercise. By the time she was done Ari could feel sweat rolling down his back from the effort it took to stay still.

Lucy registered the almost indecent bulge in the sheet covering his lap and her throat went dry.

'Your bra,' he said hoarsely. 'Take it off too.'

Lucy reached around behind her and felt for the clasp. She had to pull the bra tighter in the motion it took to undo it, and she saw Aristotle's Adam's apple move convulsively as he registered the movement. The clasp was undone, and Lucy held it for a long moment…*this was it*. And then, with an almost defiant movement, she pulled it away and threw it down, releasing her heavy breasts. She stood before him in nothing but her silk and lace pants. In some dim and distant part of her still-functioning brain Lucy had *no idea* how she was doing this—the enormity of the moment was too huge to contemplate—but the beat of her blood was drowning out everything but the need to be here right now, *with him*.

His eyes seemed to glaze over as he looked at her, making her skin tighten and tingle all over, especially her breasts. She could feel the tips puckering and growing unbearably tight. She didn't have time to feel self-conscious. Aristotle reached out with two hands and grabbed hers in both of his, pulling her close to the bed. The sheet moved down. Lucy had a stomach clenching view of narrow hips and dark hair just above—

With a smooth move she never saw coming he tumbled her down, so that she lay flat on her back. He loomed, huge and dark over her, his hands still capturing hers, held against her belly, his knuckles brushing the sensitive undersides of her breasts. Her heart was beating so fast she felt dizzy, but then his head was lowering to hers, his mouth slanting over hers, and within seconds dizziness had been replaced with heat and sensation. His naked torso crushed her chest. He released her hands and she instinctively wound them around his neck as she arched voluptuously towards him.

Never had she imagined feeling like this. This rightness. She fitted him; he fitted her. The moment she ached for him to touch her somewhere he touched her; the moment she wanted him to deepen the kiss he deepened it—sucking her tongue deep, biting her lip, pressing fiery kisses down over her jaw and further, until he hovered teasingly over her breasts.

He cupped one and then the other, caressing their firm smoothness. Lucy's breathing was fractured, jerky. She looked down but couldn't bear the eroticism of seeing her breasts in his hands like that. So she closed her eyes and cried out when he took one burning nipple into his mouth and sucked hard, rolling the tip, flicking it with his tongue, grazing it with his teeth before suckling hard again.

Lucy was burning up, her hands in his hair as he cupped both the voluptuous mounds together, his mouth tasting and testing each peak until they were throbbing with arousal.

'Please…' she begged brokenly.

Her hips moved in a silent and primeval rhythm, her lower body on fire. She looked down to see Aristotle looking up at her, eyes dark green, cheeks flushed. His huge broad shoulders blocked out the light as he finally released her breasts and came over her on strong arms, lean and awe-inspiring.

'Are you ready?'

She nodded jerkily. She wanted to say yes to anything this man said, not even caring what he meant.

'Are you sure? I think we should check, just in case…don't you?'

'Yes,' Lucy gasped. 'Whatever—just do it…'

He smiled down at her even as she registered that the sheet had fallen away and his powerful erection nudged her belly. On pure instinct she reached down and covered him with her hand, heat suffusing her face and neck as she registered the size of him—fully aroused.

He grimaced as her hand tightened on him and he took it gently away. 'That's why we have to see if you're ready Lucy, *mou*…patience.'

She didn't know what *mou* meant, but then he disappeared, and Lucy gave a yelp when she felt him drawing her pants down, over her hips and down her legs, before he spread her legs apart with big hands. Lucy tried to resist the movement, which felt far too intimate, but he was ruthless, eyes on hers, holding her, *telling her to trust him* as his head lowered. She closed her eyes and put a fist to her mouth to hold back the groan when she felt his breath feather in the intimate space between her legs, and then the sensation of his mouth and tongue on her nearly sent her shooting into the stars.

He licked her, exploring her secret folds, thrusting deep into her, circling and sucking on her clitoris until her hips were lifting off the bed, wantonly jerking towards him, her teeth biting down on her fist.

When she felt two fingers slide deep into her slick heat everything in her body teetered on an edge that she'd never known before; every nerve pulled tight. But then he was withdrawing for a moment. She heard a drawer slam shut, a foil wrapper, and then he was back over her, strong, hair-roughened thighs parting her own smoother ones even more.

She could feel his erection nudging her down there, where she burned. He moved back and forth, drawing his penis along the moistened and plump folds of her sex, eliciting a deep groan from somewhere deep within her. She was almost mindless for the need for *something*…she wasn't sure what it was…it hovered just out of reach.

Lucy put her hands on his shoulders. They glistened with sweat, and the feeling of something so earthy made her rejoice.

'Ari…' she breathed. 'Please—I'm ready.'

And that was when Ari's control broke. He heard her husky words, felt her tip her hips up towards him, reach down to take hold of him, forcing him to impale her slightly. And then he drove in deep and hard, knowing instinctively that this woman was made for him alone and they would fit like a glove.

Ari stilled his movements—both of them did. Lucy's eyes were wide with shock at the sensation of him filling her, but it wasn't painful…it was delicious.

She moved again, experimentally, and Aristotle sank into her even more, pushing her down into the bed. Lucy wrapped one leg around his waist and threw her head back, hands still clinging onto his shoulders as he slowly withdrew and then impaled her again. He continued with his slow, voluptuous rhythm, the pleasure building and building. Lucy could feel her body starting to shake as he took her other leg and bent it back, opening her up to him even more, changing the angle slightly, going even deeper, and as his movements started to get faster and more urgent Lucy could feel the onset of some-thing so huge, so terrifying as it came hurtling towards her, that she tensed—even though everything in her was urging her to meet it head-on.

Aristotle bent his head, his body holding her suspended

with his movements, and kissed her deeply. Her breasts were crushed against his chest, her arms clasping his neck. 'Let go, Lucy… It's OK…let go.'

Holding on tight, she took the final, terrifying leap and let go…and was thrown so high and so far on the wave of her orgasm that she was hardly even aware of Aristotle's own explosive loss of control as his big powerful body jerked and still rhythmically thrust into hers as the never-ending ripples of her orgasm held him suspended in a halfway world he'd never known before.

CHAPTER SEVEN

ARISTOTLE was running away. And the fact that he was aware of what he was doing made him nearly incandescent with rage. He didn't *run away*. And yet after last night, with Lucy, all he'd known was that he needed space—and fast. His brain was still too hot and far too tangled to even pretend he could deal with a banal morning-after scenario. He'd received a call from his New York PA while Lucy lay sleeping, and on the flimsiest of pretexts had declared he'd fly over for the weekend to take care of something that ordinarily he wouldn't have touched with a bargepole.

Lucy had woken to find him dressing that morning. He'd seen her wake through the reflection of the mirror as he'd knotted his tie with unsteady hands. Unsteady because he'd wanted to strip off all his confining garments and go over to where she lay in such gloriously voluptuous naked abandon and take her all over again. But the truth was he wasn't sure if he could take that intensity of experience again.

Wasn't sure if he could take that intensity of experience again? Ari's hand clenched around the crystal glass, the design digging into his palm as he looked unseeingly out of the plane window. Since when had sleeping with a woman been too intense for him? *They* were the ones left weak and dizzy and sated. Not him.

He closed his eyes and threw his head back. And then opened them again abruptly when all he could see was Lucy's passion-glazed eyes as she'd looked up at him the moment he'd filled her, the moment he'd been completely sheathed in her hot moist warmth… It had felt…it had felt like nothing he could have imagined. He could remember the feel of her breasts pushing against him, their peaks as hard as bullets against his chest, could hear their heartbeats even now, thudding slow and unsteady, and then, as he'd started to thrust deeper and deeper, the beats had got faster…until—

Aristotle swore softly. He needed to numb that *intensity*.

His mouth twisted and he called himself all sorts of a fool for running away. So it was the best sex he'd ever had? That was it. It didn't mean anything. It hadn't touched any part of him that hadn't been touched before. *So why did it feel as if it had*?

Ari blocked out that assertion. He was immune to feeling, immune to emotions. He'd started to shut them away when his mother had died, and then when Helen Savakis had come into his life, and then finally on that first night in a cold boarding school in England at the age of five. It was the last time he'd cried and now… His gut clenched. *Now he only cried in his sleep*. He reiterated it to himself: he didn't *do* emotions.

Perhaps he'd sensed that Lucy did, and that was why he'd run. A sense of calm stole over him. That was it. She wasn't like the women he went for…she was bound to be less versed in how this would work. He'd seen the look on her face that morning, slightly nervous, biting her lip… And suddenly he was right back to square one—a raging erection pushing against his trousers, thirty thousand feet in the air, and the only chance of alleviating it far behind him on Greek soil.

He just had to lay it on the line with her, that was all. Make sure she knew what not to expect. And then…then he would take her again, and these demons would not be hovering over his shoulders. Ari smiled cynically. Who would have thought he'd be growing a conscience now, after all these years?

Lucy had got over Aristotle's abrupt and cold departure yesterday morning. She told herself stoutly that she was back on an even keel. But if she allowed images to surface for a second— She stumbled slightly in the street and a kindly old woman caught her arm and smiled up at her, saying something in Greek. Lucy smiled weakly and mumbled something back. So much for an even keel. If she even *thought* about the other night for a second she lost her balance… Self-disgust ran through her.

She spied a taverna on the other side of the street and made her way there, sitting gratefully in an empty chair. She ordered sparkling water and fanned herself with a menu, thinking that perhaps it was the heat getting to her. Who was she kidding? The heat was getting to her all right, but it had nothing to do with the sun.

And along with the heat was a lingering hurt—Lucy brutally cut off her thoughts there. She wasn't hurt. *She wasn't.*

She tried to focus on her surroundings, the pretty and quaint area of Anafiotika, a hidden gem of old Athens within touristy Plaka, just beneath the Acropolis. She'd climbed up there earlier, the exertion doing little to clear her head of the tangled knots. She took a sip of water, but with annoying precision her mind slipped back again to that excruciating moment when she'd woken the day before.

She'd felt so heavy, so lethargic, so replete. She'd lazily stretched and opened one eye before realising that she was naked, and that muscles ached where no muscle had been before. In an instant she'd been alert, and staring into the cool, wide-awake green eyes of Aristotle as he'd knotted his tie in the mirror.

She needn't have worried about the embarrassment of the morning after as he'd coolly informed her he had to go to New York urgently on business, that he didn't need her, and that he'd be back late on Sunday. It was almost as if nothing had happened. Lucy had even wondered for a paralysing moment if she'd sleep-walked into her boss's bed and he was merely being diplomatic and ignoring the *faux pas*.

And then he'd gone, leaving her there, shell-shocked, the only evidence that anything had happened in the tremors that had started through her body along with the ache when she moved.

After he'd left her mind had gone to some numb place where she wouldn't have to process what had happened, answer the questions that were piling up. Was that it? Had he just been scratching an itch? Would things revert to normal now? Was he that cold with everyone? Lucy had remembered the way he'd treated Augustine Archer and she'd doubled over in her steaming shower, feeling sick. *How could she have let this happen with a man like that*?

Because, she realised now, as the everyday hustle and bustle went on around her, she simply had not had a choice. He'd overwhelmed her—her response had overwhelmed her. And she was grateful for the space and time to process what had happened.

At that moment a group of handsome young Greek men passed her table, and they all turned to look Lucy over appreciatively as they backed down the street. One of them cheekily wolf-whistled. The shock of the attention when she wasn't used to it made her freeze. She felt acutely self-conscious in her khaki shorts and V-necked black T-shirt. The waiter in the restaurant bustled over and shouted something at the boys. They ran, laughing, and he started apologising to Lucy, but she assured him smilingly that it was fine and put some money on the table, getting up to go.

She had to acknowledge as she walked away that it wasn't an entirely unpleasant experience to be noticed like that. She'd hidden away for so long that she'd never had a chance to just play with situations like this.

The sun beat down and she tipped her head up to it for a moment. She felt an alien sensation of lightness, as if she were finally letting go of a weight. It was also a sense of freedom, and she desperately wanted to cling onto it. One thing she knew: *if* Aristotle thought they could take up where they'd left off when he returned, that sense of freedom might disappear. She'd indulged in the experience once; it would have to be enough. She knew too much about him, about his cold methods, and she knew that she didn't have the hide of someone like Augustine Archer to be able to take it.

But she had a mortifying, sickening feeling that he'd had enough already, and it killed her to admit to feeling other than overjoyed at the prospect.

She set off back in the direction of the hotel. Just before she rounded the corner a flash of movement caught her eye, and she looked over to see Aristotle lounging against an ancient wall, hands thrust deep into jeans pockets, a faded white T-shirt making him look indecently handsome. Dark glasses hid those amazing eyes, but added to the overall devastating package.

It was so like something she might have conjured up out of a fantasy that she blinked and blinked again. *Was* it a mirage? He was dressed more casually than she'd ever seen him. He moved, strolled towards her. Stopped in front of her. Her heart stopped and kick-started again with heavy thuds.

This was no mirage.

'You're…back.' Despite the drink of water, Lucy's mouth felt like a desert.

Ari smiled a hard smile and in that second Lucy knew it was him. Despite his hardness something melted inside her, all her good intentions of moments ago disappearing like pathetic wisps of cloud.

He lifted his glasses onto his head. 'I left New York in the middle of the night.'

The shock of seeing him like this and the force of those eyes on hers made her brain feel fuzzy. 'But you…you had to work.'

'I sorted it out. I needed to get back here.' *I shouldn't have left,* he surprised himself thinking, as lust slammed into his gut.

'You did?' Lucy was mesmerised by his mouth, remembering what it had felt like on her skin. Heat bloomed between her legs. People jostled past them and Aristotle took her arm and led her to the side, to the wall. He pushed her back against it and stood close—far too close. She could feel him, smell him… God, she wanted to taste him.

'Ari…'

He bent his head, feathering a kiss to her neck. 'Yes, say that again. That's why I came back.'

'*Ari.*'

His hands rested on either side of her head, his pelvis was tight against hers, and she could feel how aroused he was— right here in the middle of the street, with people passing by.

'I'm going insane for you, Lucy.'

Lucy opened her mouth, but her words were stolen by his lips coming down hard and swift, demanding and eliciting a flash-fire of response. After a long drugging moment Ari lifted his head, his eyes glittering down into hers. Amazingly, she could see herself reflected in his eyes, looking up, dazed, and that sent sanity rushing back. Somehow, with superhuman strength, Lucy found the will to put her hands against his broad chest and push.

He budged only minutely, a frown drawing those black brows together.

'*No.*' Lucy was starting to panic. The speed with which he'd appeared and made her conveniently forget all logic was making her burn inside.

He quirked a devilish smile. 'You're right. Here isn't the place.'

He took her hand and started to pull her away, clearly misinterpreting her reasons for wanting to stop. Lucy dug her heels in and pulled her hand back. He didn't let go, just looked back impatiently when she wasn't moving.

'What—?'

He took one look at Lucy's mutinous face and it sent something cold through him. 'I'm sorry—did I misunderstand? Maybe you *want* to be made love to in front of Athens strollers and their families?'

'I don't want to be made love to, full-stop,' Lucy hissed, very conscious of the stares they were getting—primarily from admiring women.

Ari gripped her hand tight and Lucy, very reluctantly, let herself be pulled towards him.

Ari was frowning again slightly, something like ennui trickling through him, making him feel absurdly disappointed. 'If this is about the way I left…'

Lucy emitted a sharp laugh that disguised the dart of pain and the surge of anger at how easily she'd given in to his charm and fallen into his bed the other night. Faced with him now, the fact that she desired him even more acutely was making her regret it all the more fiercely. 'Of course it's not. I'm well aware of how you conduct yourself… I guess—oh, I don't know—I expected at least a bunch of flowers. After all, isn't that what you give all your one-night stands?'

He stood stock still, staring down at her, the lines in his face tightening and growing harsher by the minute.

'Well, let's make this more than a one-night stand, and then you'll get a priceless piece of jewellery. Is that what it'll take, Lucy?'

He looked around for a moment and spotted something Lucy didn't see. With that tight grip on her hand, he began hauling her away again. Trepidation slithered down her spine. He'd looked ready to throttle her.

He growled back, 'Tell you what—why don't we cover all bases now? That way we're clear, left in no doubt as to where we stand, because to be perfectly honest I don't think I'm going to be satisfied with just two nights.'

'What—?'

Ari stopped abruptly at a flower stall and picked out the biggest bunch of flowers the man had. Then, to Lucy's horror and the flower stall man's delight, Ari presented it to her with a mocking flourish.

Lucy took them purely because she couldn't *not*. She pasted a smile on her face for the benefit of the flower seller, and after paying Ari was leading her away again. The flowers were huge and cumbersome. Lucy tried to get his attention, pulling on his hand, but it would have been easier talking to a block of wood. He led her relentlessly through a veritable maze of streets until they emerged into a charming square and Lucy spotted shops with designer names.

Again without pausing for a moment, Ari tugged Lucy along until she found him leading her into an exclusive jewellery store, the iconic name of which made horror slam into her. As the door hissed quietly closed behind them, and the security guard clearly recognised Aristotle Levakis, Lucy tugged fiercely on Ari's hand—but to no avail. He led her over to where an eager assistant, already smelling a large sale, stood.

He drew Lucy in close to his side with an arm of steel and sent her a devotedly loving look. Only Lucy was aware of the hard glitter behind it. Hardly breaking that eye contact, he said, 'I'd like to buy something for this beautiful woman.' He flicked a glance at the sales assistant and smiled urbanely. 'Although I'm sure you'll agree that there couldn't possibly be anything in this shop to rival her beauty.'

The sales assistant cleared her throat obsequiously and looked Lucy up and down, taking in the T-shirt and shorts, the flat gladiator sandals and dusty feet. Lucy cringed from head to toe under the snooty woman's scrutiny, and right then she hated Ari more than she'd ever hated anyone in her life, hearing his well-practised patter.

Hellbent on proving *something*, Ari was still so incensed that he dragged Lucy from display to display, forcing her to look at priceless bracelets, necklaces, earrings and brooches. Every now and then she tried to entreat him, to tug on his hand, but he ignored her. A heavy mass of dark, twisted emotion was weighing him down inside.

Why hadn't her eyes lit up when they'd got in here? And *why* had he felt that punch to his solar plexus in the street when he'd believed her to be exactly the same as every other woman? And *why* was she contradicting that now, insisting on leaving? Making him feel confused and out of his depth. He heard her speak again.

'Ari. *Please.* Let's just go. I don't want anything here.'

He turned to look down, and the stunning natural beauty of her face and those stormy grey eyes nearly floored him. He could feel the thrust of her soft breasts against his chest. She looked pale. But he did not know how to get himself out of this situation except by saying, his voice harder than he'd ever heard it, 'We're not leaving until you choose something, Lucy. There's not a woman in the world who would say no to that, so please don't play the wide-eyed innocent with me. It won't work.'

Lucy's belly clenched at the look of pure cynicism that

crossed Ari's features, twisting them. Suddenly her anger dissolved, and all she felt was sad. She tore her eyes away and looked around futilely, hating every single item of jewellery on display. This whole scenario was making her skin crawl. But she knew he meant it. They would not leave until she'd chosen something.

She tugged her hand, and for the first time Ari let go. Moving away, feeling tears film her eyes, Lucy searched and searched, barely even seeing the glittering gems arrayed in glorious profusion.

But then something did catch her eye, hidden away at the back of one of the cabinets. It was a necklace of such stunning simplicity that it took her breath away. It was a butterfly design; she'd always had a sentimental thing about butterflies, and her mother had used to buy her presents with butterfly motifs. Seeing this now was like some kind of sign, and Lucy had to fight back the tears.

The wings of the design glistened with what she could only assume were tiny diamonds, and three delicate silver strands linked it on each side to the catch.

She pointed with a trembling finger. 'I like that one.'

A startled gasp of disbelief came from the sales assistant, clearly seeing her month's worth of commission disappearing down the drain.

'*That* one?'

Ari had heard the exchange and was behind Lucy, looking over her shoulder. She tensed as the fine hairs stood up on the back of her neck.

The sales assistant couldn't keep the pain out of her voice. 'Well, yes, it is a nice piece…' She laughed nervously, 'If you like something more…subtle…and the designer is local. But *really*…'

Lucy heard a scathing, 'Less than one thousand euros? I don't think so…' come from behind her, and then she felt his mouth close to her ear, so only she could hear which he said. 'I think I want a lot more than a two-night stand Lucy, *mou*, so I think you're worth a lot more than that…'

Before she knew it Ari had arrogantly picked out a completely different necklace, with a huge sapphire stone surrounded by diamonds, and the ecstatic sales assistant was wrapping it up efficiently before they changed their minds.

Outside the shop, Lucy broke desperately from Ari's grasp, but he caught her again effortlessly and swung her round. She closed her eyes and to her utter horror could feel tears welling. She couldn't stop one from slipping out. She felt a tense stillness come into his body.

'Lucy…' He sounded exasperated now. Lucy didn't doubt that he'd moved women to tears after buying them jewellery before, but for entirely different reasons.

Ari took hold of Lucy's arms. They felt slender and fragile under his hands. He saw the tear slip down the pale softness of her cheek and cursed himself silently, feeling like an absolute heel when he didn't even know why. He'd just spent a fortune on her! And in his experience money equalled a satisfied woman. He was floundering badly, had never been in this place before, and had certainly never expected a reaction like *this*. She looked almost green.

Seeing her still holding onto that crazy bunch of flowers, Ari grabbed them out of her hand and passed them to a woman strolling past. He was unaware of her gasp of delighted surprise as she took them, entirely focused on Lucy again. More tears were slipping down her cheeks. He was used to women's histrionics, but this was different. She was doing it so silently. And he could tell that she hated that she was crying.

'Lucy…look—'

She seemed to come to life and lifted a hand, knocking aside one of his as she wiped her cheek. Finally she opened her eyes, and their swirling depths made him want to pull her close. But everything about her screamed *stay back*.

Her voice was heart-achingly husky. 'I've never been so hu...humiliated in all my life.'

Ari raked a hand through his hair. He wanted to go back to when he'd seen Lucy in the street, taken her in his arms and kissed her, and start all over again. But when she'd pushed him away and then said those things about the flowers he'd lost all perspective. Without wanting to look too closely at why, he just knew it had something to do with her reference to those other women. That this was exactly the same... A small voice crowed, *Wasn't it?*

Lucy couldn't look up at Ari any more. She broke free and started to walk back towards the hotel. She could see it in the distance; they were closer than she'd thought. She felt numb.

When she felt Ari take her hand again she stopped dead and took a deep breath before turning around. 'Look—'

'No, *you* look.'

She did—right up at him, emotion still swirling danger-ously in her breast. She'd never felt so vulnerable, like every one of her childhood fears was being taken out and exposed to the harsh sunlight.

Ari felt tight. 'Those women in London—the flowers... They weren't one-night stands. They were pathetic attempts to negate your effect on me and to keep up appearances.' His mouth twisted. 'I'd agreed with Parnassus that it might help distract people from investigating the merger if I was seen to be out and about as usual.'

Lucy's head went into mind-melt.

'I'm sorry for leaving you so abruptly the other morning. I'm sorry for the flowers, and I'm sorry for dragging you into that shop and forcing you to choose something you didn't want.' *Even now he couldn't understand her reaction, or why he was explaining himself when he never had before.* And he couldn't really believe he'd felt compelled to defend his actions in London. But he wanted Lucy more than he wanted to understand right then…

Fresh tears threatened and Lucy wailed inwardly, *Don't be nice! I can't handle nice.*

She pursed her lips even as her anger drained away spectacularly. *He hadn't slept with those women?* She felt very wobbly and vulnerable, and knew her words lacked impact. 'Your behaviour was unforgivable. Spending that kind of money just to make a point is disgusting.'

His face tightened. He held up the bag. 'What do you want me to do with it?'

Lucy felt wrong-footed by his immediate response. The Ari she'd thought she knew was morphing out of all recognition. She thought for a second. 'I don't think that lady in the shop deserves commission when she couldn't be bothered to promote local talent. I don't know…it'd be nice to give it to someone who'd really appreciate…'

She looked around. In the thronged square, back at the jeweller's shop, she could see a young couple clearly in love, looking wistfully through the window at the engagement rings. Lucy could see the pain on the young man's face at his girlfriend's quickly disguised yet crestfallen expression as they walked away. She glanced up at Ari and could see that he had followed her gaze and witnessed the little exchange.

She saw his jaw clench. He let her hand go and strode through the crowd to the young couple. Lucy saw the conversation, saw Ari gesture back to her with a rueful smile and hand the young man the elaborately wrapped box. The young couple's faces were shocked as Ari walked back to Lucy and took her hand again.

He led her away, but looked back for a moment and said, 'Satisfied now?'

Lucy nodded jerkily. She couldn't quite believe he'd done

that, and asked a little shakily, 'How…how much was it worth?'

He tossed back a figure and she felt the colour drain from her face. She bit her lip and said quietly, 'Oh, well, it'll buy them a nice engagement ring…or three.'

She felt the earth shift as she realised she was seeing a completely different side to Ari. She was very much afraid that she'd stuck her head into the lion's mouth and he was about to bite down—hard.

By the middle of the following week Lucy was as drunk as she'd ever felt, and all without touching a drop of alcohol. She couldn't stop her mind drifting back to last Sunday afternoon, now as she sat waiting for Ari to come out of a private meeting with Parnassus being held in his villa in the hills above Athens.

When they'd got back to the hotel an unspoken inevitability had vibrated between them, intensifying the closer they'd got to her room. Once inside, as if to stave it off, as if she could save herself from the burning flames, Lucy had said breathlessly, 'Wait…what is this now? What are we?'

Ari had rested back against the door, hands behind him, those lean hips in the low-slung jeans making Lucy's mouth dry and her head ache with the effort it took not to look down.

'We are two consenting adults, exploring a strong mutual attraction, and this is…the second time we make love.'

Heat had exploded all around her. He'd pushed off the door and come towards her. Lucy had put out a hand, as if that could stop him, and had watched as he'd nonchalantly stripped off his T-shirt.

She'd swallowed. 'But…what about us…working together? How can we do this…?'

He'd caught up with her effortlessly and pulled her into him, tight. She had felt the bulge of his arousal pressing against his jeans, pressing just above the apex of her thighs, and her legs had nearly buckled.

He'd bent his head and whispered at the corner of her mouth, '*This is* how we do this...'

Things had escalated swiftly. Clothes pulled and yanked, they'd stumbled and staggered towards the bed, Lucy falling back into the softness, somehow naked except for her underwear.

She'd watched as Ari yanked down his jeans and briefs in one go. She'd gazed at him in all his bronzed, aroused glory, she'd realised in that moment that ever since that day she'd bumped into him in the lift *this* image had been hidden deep in the recesses of her darkest fantasies. A fantasy she never might have acknowledged if this man hadn't wanted her too.

Was that why he'd got under her skin so thoroughly from the start? The revelation sent her pulse soaring, pounding through her veins and under her skin, even now, as she sat on the chair with her legs tight together and Parnassus' own assistant sitting just feet away.

Even that couldn't halt the images, though. Ari had come towards her like an avenging god and pushed her legs apart, where they dangled over the bed. On two hands he'd rested over her. After looking down at her for an intensely long moment, he'd pushed down one bra strap and then the other, and then pulled down the cups of her black bra so that her breasts were exposed, upthrust by the confining underwire.

When he'd bent his head to blow softly Lucy had groaned deep in her throat, in between her legs a deep, endless ache. When his tongue had flicked out and teasingly licked around the rapidly hardening peak of one breast she'd arched her back, willing him to suck it deep, like he had before.

When he hadn't, she'd looked at him, felt sweat breaking out on her brow. He'd smiled devilishly, and she'd cursed him silently, her eyes flashing in a mute appeal.

He'd shifted her back onto the bed and with far too prac-
tised ease managed to dispense with her bra. His big hands
on her thighs had held her apart. He'd looked at her with such
desirous intensity she'd felt trepidation lick through her,
feeling that she *had* to be imagining this.

She'd spoken huskily, and winced now at the memory.
'How can you…how can you find me attractive? I'm not
like… I'm too big…I'm *plump*…'

He'd merely hooked fingers into the side of her pants,
said throatily, 'You're perfect…' and started to pull them
down, dropping them summarily on the floor. He'd stood
again, blatantly aroused, making a mockery of her words.
Making her feel as if she was all woman and the only woman
for him.

He'd bent over her and she'd felt his erection teasing her,
hot and hard against her desire-drenched sex. She'd felt so
wanton, but had bitten her lip and forced herself not to move
her hips towards him as she'd wanted to do so very badly.

Lying right over her, so she could feel his chest against her,
he'd stretched her arms above her head, the movement causing
her breasts to rise as if offered to him like succulent desserts.

Holding her hands captive with one of his much larger
ones, he'd trailed his other hand down the side of her body,
teasing the side of one breast, and whispered in her ear, 'You
are quite simply the pure embodiment of my every fantasy of
what the perfect feminine form is… I didn't know it till I saw
you, and now I can see nothing else…'

Lucy's heart had stopped altogether. She'd searched his
eyes as he'd lifted back and looked down, so dark and hot
they'd scorched her alive.

'You…really mean that?'

Lucy hoped desperately now that she hadn't sounded as
vulnerable as she'd felt in that moment.

In answer Ari had bent his head and laved one of her nipples with his mouth and tongue, before sucking it deep, causing her back to arch again helplessly.

Releasing her hands for only a second while he'd put on protection, he'd come back and captured them high again. Lucy's hips had bucked of their own volition.

He'd then slid into her, inch by torturous inch, and when he was in as far as he could go, when she didn't know where she started or he ended, he'd leant close to her mouth and kissed her deeply, before saying, so quietly that she almost didn't hear, 'Yes…I really mean it.'

And then, with slow, deep thrusts which built and built to a stunning crescendo—

The door in front of Lucy opened suddenly, and she jumped up at the same time as Parnsassus' assistant, a guilty flush staining her cheeks, breathing as if she'd just been running. A pulse throbbed between her legs and she was caught by a pair of glittering green eyes.

She saw Ari smile sardonically, as if he knew *exactly* what she'd just been thinking about, and Lucy flushed even redder. He strolled over and took the file she was holding out of her hands, his fingers caressing hers underneath for a lingering moment, making her pulse beat even faster.

Lucy nearly groaned out loud, and then he said *sotto voce*, 'Have Helios bring the car round. We'll be out of here in less than ten minutes… I'll tell Parnassus we can work from my office for the rest of the afternoon.'

Lucy just nodded, not capable of much else, and certainly not capable of anything like *work*. She felt feverish, distracted, more elated than she'd ever felt, and knew that right now she had neither the strength of will *nor the inclination* to resist this man.

* * *

'We've been invited to my father's house for dinner on Friday night.'

'You mean *you've* been invited for dinner.' Lucy shuddered inwardly, she didn't fool herself for a second in thinking that Helen Levakis had included her in that cosy little invitation.

Ari shook his head and marvelled at this woman in front of him. They were having a private dinner in her bedroom at the hotel, late in the evening. She looked so beautiful in just a bathrobe, with her dark hair spread around her shoulders, not a scrap of make-up, that delicious cleavage just visible in the gap of her robe. When he thought of how they'd barely made it back to the office the afternoon before— He stopped his rampant mind. He was far too susceptible to this woman. And, worryingly, he didn't feel at all complacent or triumphant about the fact that he'd got her into bed. If anything he just felt a growing sense of hunger. The fact that that was not the usual way for him and women was conveniently pushed aside. He reminded himself that Lucy was different, from a different class—world. It was the novelty of that, *that* was all. And for now he was loving the novelty.

Reaching for her hand, he tugged her up and over until she fell into his lap, making a spasm of lust arrow straight to his groin.

He shook his head, and before he bent to kiss her said, 'Where I go, you go.'

Lucy accepted the kiss, drowned in the kiss, but a sense of guilty anticipation made her shiver slightly. No matter that they were spending time together like this. Ari was still as open as a closed book when it came to anything but the most general conversation. And now the thought of getting a chance to learn more about this man, who was fast tangling her head into one big knot of confusion and reducing her body to little more than a slave to his, was proving to be far headier than was healthy for her heart.

When the kiss deepened, and as Ari carried Lucy over to the bed and came down on top of her with his delicious weight and told her how beautiful she was, how desirable, she conveniently blocked out the clamour of voices in her head telling her to be careful, not to be weak, and not to be so easily seduced—and above all *not to fall in love*.

On Friday evening Lucy was sitting ramrod-straight on a rigid divan in the main drawing room of the grossly opulent Levakis house. Tonight had to be one of the most excruciatingly uncomfortable evenings of her life. From the moment she'd arrived, with Ari's hand on her arm, it had been clear she wasn't welcome.

Lucy had held her head high and thanked her lucky stars for her chaotic but expensive education; every time Helen had directed some snide comment her way, or had tried to undermine her, Lucy had answered with the utmost dignity. Helen had even been so rude as to conduct some of the conversation between the few guests in French, but her eyes had almost popped out of her head when Lucy had replied fluently.

Lucy felt inordinately proud of her mother's legacy.

Ari was now on the other side of the room, talking to the same beautiful blonde who'd captured his attention at that function the first week. Lucy tried to ignore the poisoned darts that seemed to be arrowing into her heart, and tensed even more when she saw Anatolios, Ari's half-brother, head her way.

He sat down, far too close for comfort, obviously drunk, and Lucy tried to edge away, smiling weakly. He merely moved with her, crowding her. She felt intensely vulnerable.

Anatolios's blue eyes followed where her gaze had just been and he said, 'Beautiful, isn't she?'

Lucy flushed. 'I'm not sure I know what you mean.'

She looked at Anatolios reluctantly. She guessed she couldn't be much older than her own twenty-three years, and hoped the revulsion she felt didn't show on her face.

He smiled sleazily, and then, shockingly, ran a fleshy finger up and down Lucy's bare arm. She flinched, but couldn't move, hemmed in as she was.

He gestured with his head. 'That's Pia Kyriapoulos. She used to be a famous model, and now she's famous for being wealthy and divorced and looking for a new husband.'

Lucy swallowed painfully and looked across the room. They did look amazing together—blonde contrasting with dark. Pia had her hand resting on Ari's arm, and he certainly didn't look in a hurry to move it. At that moment he looked up and straight at Lucy. Feeling inordinately exposed, Lucy smiled brilliantly and looked back at Anatolios as if he'd said something funny. Not as if he'd said something to make her heart feel as if it was being ripped, still beating, out of her chest.

When she felt Ari's gaze move again Lucy ripped her arm away from Anatolios, who glowered sulkily at her. His eyes dropped to her cleavage and Lucy screamed inwardly. The guy was a total creep.

Just then Helen swept into the room and said something to Ari who, after a moment's hesitation, followed her from the room, his face hard. Sensing a chance to escape, Lucy mumbled something about needing the bathroom and fled, vowing to get out of there even if she had to leave on her own.

Wherever I go, you go. Ari's words resounded mockingly in her head. At least until the next available, infinitely more beautiful woman came along, she surmised grimly.

She was coming back from the bathroom and passing a partially opened door when she heard raised voices. *Ari and Helen.*

Without being conscious of what she was doing, she slowed down and heard Ari say, a low and blistering voice,

'I'll never marry someone like her; she's completely inappropriate. And anyway, don't you think it's a little late to be doing the concerned mother act?'

CHAPTER EIGHT

LUCY'S heart froze like ice in her chest as the words registered. Was Helen afraid that their affair was more than just a fling? She had to swallow back a semi-hysterical cry, putting a hand to her mouth. Well, Ari had certainly reassured her of that.

The next words from Helen were indistinctly shrill, and then Ari's voice came again. Lucy stood rooted to the spot in some kind of sick, paralysed fascination, and heard him say something along the lines of, '…useless waste of space of a brother…'

There was an awful silence, and then the sharp crack of what could only be a hand across a cheek.

Knowing that it wouldn't have been Ari, and acting on a surge of adrenalin that was pure primal instinct, Lucy pushed open the door and flew into the room, aiming herself straight at Helen, who still had her hand raised, her eyes glittering almost feverishly.

Lucy was unaware of their shocked looks. She saw only Ari's proud stance, the livid handprint and the trickle of blood from the corner of his mouth. She saw red, and for the first and only time in her life considered striking another person. It was only Ari's quick reflex action, pulling her back behind him, that stopped her.

Helen lowered her hand and her eyes took on a malevolent glow. She smiled cruelly. 'Well, well—if it isn't the quiet little secretary, come to save her lover.' The woman's obsidian eyes flicked up and down and she added cuttingly, 'Or perhaps I shouldn't say *little*.'

Lucy made to move again and Ari held her firm, glancing back with a hard expression, 'Leave it, Lucy.'

He turned back, and Lucy could feel the ice in his gaze even though he wasn't looking at her.

'She wouldn't balk at striking you too. After all, you never had any qualms about striking a five-year-old—did you, Helen?'

Helen's focus moved back to Ari, and Lucy could see the older woman's face grow mottled with anger. Abruptly Ari turned and pulled Lucy with him, and within a blur of minutes they were sitting in the back of his car, leaving the house behind.

Lucy was still shaking, a mixture of powerful anger and shock coursing through her. She glanced at Ari. He was looking resolutely out of the window. When she saw his mouth her heart lurched painfully.

'You…you're bleeding.'

He turned abruptly, and the dead look in his eyes scared her. He smiled harshly. 'Want to kiss it better for me, Lucy?'

He flicked out a handkerchief nevertheless, and dabbed at the blood. Overcome with an emotion she couldn't name, Lucy reached out and put her hand to his cheek, where it still felt warm.

'How could she have hit you when you were so small?'

A surge of emotion so powerful that it made him tremble caused black spots to dance before Ari's eyes. His breathing grew shallow. The feel of Lucy's hand like a cooling balm on his hot cheek, the look on her face… He'd never, *ever* had someone rush to his defence so unreservedly. He'd felt the fine vibrating tremors of her anger as he'd held her back, and he didn't doubt that if he hadn't stopped her she might very well have struck Helen. The realisation was cataclysmic, earth-shattering.

A hardness entered him. He certainly wasn't going to shatter along with it. Everyone wanted something out of him—especially women. Lucy was just taking advantage of a vulnerable moment.

Lucy's wrist was gripped and pulled down. Ari's eyes glittered at her, but at least some life had come back into them. 'Quite easily,' he bit out. 'I was an easier target then.'

He kept hold of her wrist, almost painfully, but Lucy didn't say anything.

'Don't pity me, Lucy Proctor. I don't need anyone's pity.'

The fierce pride on his face nearly made Lucy weep. She shook her head and managed to pull her hand back, cradling it with her other one. He saw the movement and sighed deeply, raking his hair with barely concealed anger.

Lucy looked away for a long moment. The rest of the evening was coming back—what had happened just before she'd gone to the bathroom, and then the words she'd heard. *What was wrong with her?* Sitting here mooning over a man who quite patently needed no one and was biding his time with her until he flitted to the next woman.

She started hesitantly, 'I didn't mean to… I was just passing and heard her…'

'How did you know it wasn't me hitting *her*?' came the sardonically amused question.

Lucy turned around, a fierce expression on her face. 'Because I know you would never do anything like that.'

His belly clenched. It was harder not to touch her than to touch her and risk that emotion rising again, so Ari reached out and tugged a resisting Lucy onto his lap. He felt an unusual peace steal over him. He buried his head in her neck and after a moment felt her relax, her curves softening into him with delicious inevitability.

But then he felt her tense again, and he looked up and said with a growl, 'Stop it. Relax, Lucy, *mou*.'

She was biting her lip and avoiding his eye. He turned her jaw so that she had to face him, and she said, almost defiantly, 'I saw you with that woman. I won't…won't be some substitute. If you'd prefer to be with her, then please…just go back.'

The thought of going back to that house made Ari shudder. He'd known it would be a mistake to go at all, and hated the fact that he had done so. Hated the fact that after all these years there was still a tiny sliver of yearning left for something he'd never experienced. Harmony. Even as that thought materialised in his head he blocked it ruthlessly, focused on the woman on his lap, reducing his world to the here and now.

He shook his head, amazed that Lucy could have seen him and Pia together and not have known that he'd all but itched to go back across the room to *her*. Then he remembered the moment before Helen had come into the room and asked to speak to him. Lucy had been with Anatolios, looking at him and laughing gaily. Anatolios had been practically sitting in her lap.

Dark anger surged. 'From what I saw of you and my brother, you looked very cosy also… Are you sure it's not you who wants to go back to him?'

Lucy couldn't help the shudder of disgust run through her as she said quickly, '*No*. I was just—we were just…talking.'

The relief that surged through Ari made him feel weak. He pressed a kiss to Lucy's bare shoulder and she shivered again, but this time he recognised desire and it was heady.

'Then, please believe me, I too have no desire to go back to that house. Pia Kyriapoulos is a woman who is looking for her next wealthy protector. She thinks I could be it, but this evening I told her in no uncertain terms that I have no interest in signing up for the job. And anyway...' Ari brought Lucy's hand between them to his lap, where she could feel the stirrings of his growing arousal. 'She doesn't have this effect on me.'

Ari felt Lucy's fingers flutter over him and held back a low groan as his arousal soared. In that second he had a flash of an idea. Without stopping to consider what he was doing, he said, 'When we get back to the hotel, pack some things for the weekend. We're getting out of Athens...'

When Lucy woke the next morning she knew immediately that she was alone in the strange bed, but she was too deliciously lethargic and sated to worry about it. She heard nothing except beautiful stillness and the gentle lapping of water nearby.

They had travelled here, to this island, which Ari had told her was called Paros, by helicopter last night. It had all been a little overwhelming to Lucy. When they'd arrived Ari had driven them in a Jeep to this place, which Lucy hadn't been able to make out in the dark.

Now, without opening her eyes yet, as if superstitious for a moment that it might disappear, Lucy knew that there were doors open nearby. She could feel the warm breeze, could smell the tang of the sea and feel the bright sunlight.

Finally she opened her eyes. They took a second to adjust, and then as if in a dream she got up, blindly threw on a T-shirt and walked to the open French doors and the tiny balcony. She simply could not take in the beauty of her surroundings for a moment. The balcony seemed to be perched right over the Aegean Sea, which stretched out in glittering blue before her, other islands visible as shapes in the hazy distance under a clear cerulean sky.

The modest house was whitewashed and all but clinging onto the rocky coast, nestling alongside equally bright houses either side. Lucy frowned slightly. She'd seen Ari's portfolio of extensive properties around the world, and knew he had a luxurious villa on Santorini, but she'd never seen pictures of this house. She looked around. Admittedly, it was more humble than anything she might have expected of him. And all the more intriguing.

She heard a sound behind her and turned to see Ari, shouldering his way in through the door with arms full of supplies. Her breath snagged at remembering how he'd stripped her bare last night and taken her to heaven and back on the modest double bed. He was wearing long shorts and a faded T-shirt, and looked impossibly young and handsome at that moment—a million miles from the proud, successful, arrogant billionaire.

He pressed a lingering kiss to her mouth and proceeded to spread out a veritable feast of a breakfast on an ancient wrought-iron table. Bread, jams, fruit… Then he disappeared, presumably to the tiny kitchen downstairs, and came back with steaming fragrant coffee in two cups.

'Cat got your tongue?' he asked lightly as they sat down and Lucy still hadn't said a word.

She shook her head and tried to communicate with him what she was thinking, feeling. She made a half-gesture around them, encompassing the view. 'It's so beautiful… I can't even begin to describe…' She looked at him then. His face was shuttered, dark glasses shielding his eyes. 'This property isn't listed with your other ones…'

Ari's jaw clenched. He looked out towards the glittering Aegean. When he'd made the decision to come here he hadn't stopped to consider Lucy's reaction to the basic nature of the house. He knew very few women who wouldn't have turned up their noses and shuddered disdainfully. A ridiculous feeling of disappointment ran through him and he drawled, 'You'd prefer to be on Santorini? The villa there certainly is…larger.'

Shock coursed through Lucy. 'No! That's not what I meant at all. I'd much prefer to be here…' She hated that he'd jumped to that conclusion. 'I just mentioned it because I hadn't seen it. That's all.'

Ari flicked her a glance. 'It's not listed because I've deliberately kept it private. It was my mother's house—where she grew up.'

'Oh.' There didn't seem to be anything more to say, and Lucy could feel a wall spring up between them. Clearly he wasn't going to elaborate. It seemed important to make him believe so she leaned across and took his hand. 'Ari, I'm glad you brought me here. Really.'

After a long day in the sun, exploring the island's beaches and eating a basic picnic, drinking sparkling wine in the shade on an empty beach, making love until their bodies seemed boneless and sated, Ari couldn't stop thinking about Lucy's words and expression from that morning. She'd seemed sincere. He'd believed her to be sincere when she'd professed to liking the place.

He held her hand in his now, as they wandered through the ancient winding streets of his mother's birthplace. He repressed the urge to ask her if she'd really meant what she'd said—if she really loved this humble little place as much as she seemed to—because he hated how important it felt to him that she did.

A little later Ari sat back in his chair in the small taverna he'd brought her to, and Lucy's belly flipped over at his expression. He was looking at her so intensely she had to ask, 'What…? Have I got something on my face?'

He shook his head and smiled, and her heart turned over. She had once thought he was incapable of smiling, but the younger-seeming, softer side of this man was altogether far too enticing.

'Just a lot of freckles. Who would have known you'd freckle so easily?'

Lucy grimaced. 'I have celtic ancestry.'

He smiled wider, lounging back, cradling a half-empty wine glass. 'They're cute.'

Lucy scowled at the word. 'Unfortunately we can't all go a deeper shade of bronze in the sun.'

She tried to stop her eyes roving over his powerful form but couldn't resist. His T-shirt strained over broad shoulders and clung to that lean torso; low-slung jeans were so low slung that she could see a sliver of taut dark flesh just above the button, the dark shading of hair making her heart trip.

'Stop devouring me with your eyes, or I'll carry you back to bed over my shoulder, Lucy Proctor.'

She looked up again and blushed. He leant forward and captured her hand.

'It's amazing that you can blush when you're so incredibly sensual…when you wear such decadent underwear…'

Lucy groaned.

'…and have a body to put the Venus de Milo to shame…'

'I don't… *Stop*.' Lucy glanced around, mortified, in case someone had heard him. He laughed out loud.

'Yes, you do—and it's entirely appropriate that we're here, because this is the island that supplied the Parian marble for the sculpture.' He kept her hand and asked then, 'Tell me, Lucy, why is it that you have these two different sides? And why did you fight not to fall into my bed? Was it all a game?'

His voice had hardened, his hand had tightened, and Lucy looked at him and felt nervous. It suddenly seemed very important to be honest with him.

Even more so when he added, 'And how is it that you speak at least two other languages fluently and can hold your own in the snobby dining rooms of Athens?'

Lucy was silent for a long time. She looked out of the window that they were seated beside and saw the dark ocean, and fishing boats twinkling under a moonlit sky. And then she said haltingly, 'My mother was one of the most celebrated burlesque performers in the world...'

And before she knew it she was telling him everything, and he was listening, as rapt as she'd ever seen him. She told him about living in Paris, and before that Rio de Janeiro, New York...London. The ever-changing schools, the nomadic nature of their lives.

Lucy wrinkled her nose. 'Her real name was Mabel Proctor, but she changed it to Maxine Malbec.'

Ari frowned. His thumb stopped making little circles of sensation in her palm.

'*The* Maxine Malbec?'

Lucy nodded, feeling slightly sick. Was he going to judge her now or, worse, judge her mother? She started to pull her hand back, but he gripped it again.

He was shaking his head. 'Lucy, that's an amazing story... The picture I saw in your flat—I thought there was something familiar about her.'

She smiled wryly. 'That's what I was afraid of. And it's not a story—it was my life.' She shrugged, feeling self-conscious. 'Having a mother who was so overtly...sexual made me wary, I think, of that side of me.' Her mouth tightened. 'It's also why I have an aversion to expensive jewellery...trinkets... Seeing my mother fobbed off by so many rich men over the years... My father was one of those men, married with his own family. He had no desire for a love-child.' Lucy's voice trailed away. She was shocked she'd revealed so much so quickly.

She didn't elaborate on how precarious her life had been until she'd grown older and taken control of herself and her mother. She also didn't elaborate on the fear she still had of becoming dependent on a man, on how her father's rejection had fostered a deep feeling of insecurity she was only just beginning to let go of.

Ari winced inwardly when he recalled her reaction to his asking her to buy something for Augustine Archer, and then dragging her around that jewellery shop. He remembered the innately sexy way Lucy had stripped for him that first night. 'You've obviously inherited her natural sensuality—*that's all*. She sounds like she was an amazing woman, and it must have been hard, raising a daughter on her own.'

Lucy was struck somewhere very vulnerable by his easy understanding. She nodded and smiled weakly, feeling emotion rise. 'She was…*is* an amazing woman.'

Ari frowned. 'She's still alive?'

Lucy nodded. 'Yes, but…' She told him about her mother's illness and the home that she was now in.

He said quietly, 'It must be hard to see her like that…diminished.'

Lucy just nodded, terrified she might start crying. 'It is.'

To her relief he seemed happy to let it drop there, and discreetly paid the bill before tugging her up and leading her back down the quiet winding streets to the humble little house.

A few hours later Ari lay on his back, his arms around Lucy's sleeping form, her breasts rising and falling gently against his bare chest. Even though he was recently sated, that subtle movement made him hard again. He shifted minutely and bit back a groan when Lucy moved too, and he felt her nipples against his side like two hard berries.

For the first time in his life he'd put himself in a situation where he couldn't just get up and leave a woman behind—after all, where could he go? And for the first time it wasn't sending that usual feeling of suffocating claustrophobia into his belly.

* * *

The following evening Lucy was changing while Ari had a shower in the small bathroom downstairs. The house *was* tiny, and rustic and beyond basic, but she loved it. Ari had told her earlier of how his mother had grown up there with her sister and her mother, his grandfather having died when they were small.

She went to the balcony and smoothed the plain dark red sundress over her hips. Her skin tingled from being in the sun, and she felt freer than she'd felt in a long time. She'd called her mother's home earlier, and she was obviously having a good day—although Lucy had had to explain again why she wasn't able to visit for another week. It seemed as if her mother was making friends with some of the other residents, and the matron had assured her again that she was being well cared for. The relief was enormous.

A sound made her whirl around from where she was leaning against the balcony rail, watching the sun go down over the sea. Ari stood in the doorway with just a towel around his lean hips.

She looked up, throat dry, and met his eyes. They glowed with dark, decadent promise. He put his hand to the towel and with a flick of his wrist it was gone. Lucy's body flamed.

'Come here…' he said softly.

Lucy tried to resist the feeling of hot insanity. 'Ari, I've just changed…'

'Come *here*.'

On shaky legs and bare feet Lucy walked over and said, 'Has anyone ever told you that you're extremely bossy and arrogant?'

He shook his head and pulled her right into him, reaching for her dress and pulling it up, at the same time pulling her pants down. Excitement made Lucy shiver uncontrollably.

'Only you seem to have the nerve to say these things…' he growled, mock angrily.

And then talking stopped for a long, languorous moment.

* * *

Much later, when the moon had risen and the stars were out, they headed out for dinner. Lucy had put on a light cardigan as the late spring evening had a slightly cool edge. Her eyes drank Ari in as she trailed him, her hand firmly clasped in his. She never would have imagined him to be so tactile, but he was always reaching out to touch her, to take her hand, rub the back of his hand down a cheek... She sighed inwardly. He was wearing black trousers and a snowy white shirt, and he was more gorgeous than any one man had a right to be.

This part of northern Paros was a sleepy fishing village. The summer hordes hadn't descended yet, but in the distance Lucy heard music and recognised a traditional Greek tune as they rounded the corner into an idyllic little square where a taverna was all lit up. A mad profusion of flowers erupted from every windowsill and around the door.

Lucy heard shouts and laughter, and as they went in Ari ducked his head to avoid hitting the doorframe. An even bigger shout went up, and suddenly a crowd was thronging around them and a huge man was dragging Ari's face down and kissing him soundly.

When he could, Ari pulled Lucy forward, feeling an incredible lightness in his chest. He'd missed coming here. A gut-wrenching sense of homecoming nearly floored him with its intensity. London and the merger and Athens and Helen all seemed to be light years away from this moment.

But as if he couldn't hold it down the thought rose up like a spectre: *the emotion...* The threat of it was rising up to swallow him whole. That was why he hadn't been back.

He felt for Lucy's luscious curves and let her distract him from those dark thoughts, introducing her to his mother's old friends and even to some distant cousins. He could see a few of the young bucks eyeing her up, but with one warning look from him they retreated, shamefaced. Ari kept her close when they were seated in the corner with Costas, the owner, who pulled up a chair and ordered a veritable feast on their behalf.

Lucy sat back a while later and groaned, wiping her mouth with a napkin, 'I've never eaten as much as I have these last two days. And I do *not* need any extra padding.'

Ari looked at Lucy from under hooded lids, his eyes drifting down to that delectable cleavage in her red dress. It made him remember taking that dress off her only hours before, unhooking her bra and letting those voluptuous mounds spill into his hands. His body tightened and grew hot with annoying predictability. She turned him on with such ease...

She caught his eye and smiled and leant forward, crossing her arms so that her breasts were pushed together and forward. 'See something you like?'

Ari's green gaze glittered and darkened. He leant forward too and said softly, 'Witch. I'll punish you for that.'

They looked at each other, everything fading into the background for a long intense moment, until Costas came over and pulled Ari up, breaking the spell. It was only then that Lucy saw the tables and chairs had been pushed back, the volume of music had been raised and Ari stood now with Costas, arms high, as they started to do a mesmeric Greek dance.

Lucy's breath caught in her throat. It was so beautiful. It should have made Ari look effeminate, but it did the opposite. A couple of the older ladies dressed in black got up and danced with the men, their steps in sync as the music started to increase in tempo. As more people, young and old, joined in and linked arms, the music got faster and faster. The next thing Lucy knew she was being hauled up to join in.

She hissed at Ari. 'Don't you *dare*.'

But he didn't listen, just drew her into the melee, and Lucy found herself laughingly trying to keep up with everyone else. The women were showing her the complex steps, it was frantic and captivating, and as the last evocative chords died away she stumbled right into Ari's arms.

Something potent and silent was vibrating between them, and without further ado Ari grabbed Lucy's cardigan and they left, a silent intensity surrounding them all the way until they returned to the small house. Barely had the door closed before their mouths were fused, hands seeking desperately to touch bare flesh. They didn't even make it up the stairs. Ari took her there and then, fast and furiously.

It was only later, after they'd made it to the bed and made love again, that Lucy woke from a tangled dream to a strange sound. She was curled close to Ari's big body and she looked up to see that he had an arm flung over his face. His breathing was fast and shallow and he was speaking in Greek.

Lucy put her hand on his arm, tried to draw it down, and it was only when she did that that she saw the tracks of tears on his face. Her heart turned over.

At her light touch, he was awake in an instant, eyes alert, straight on hers. Lucy's voice was incredibly husky. 'You were...' She faltered, nearly saying *crying* but instinctively stopping herself. 'You were having a dream...you sounded upset.'

He did nothing for a moment, and then his face closed over and became so cold she nearly shivered. His expression was quite clear in the bright moonlight streaming in through the open doors.

In an instant he'd jackknifed off the bed to go and stand with his back to her at the balcony railing, looking out to the dark expanse of the sea. He was naked, and his physique was so gloriously powerful that it took Lucy's breath away for a moment. He was also extremely tense.

She got up and pulled on a T-shirt, went over silently to stand next to him. She noticed that his hands were wrapped so tight around the railing that his knuckles shone white.

Instinctively she put her hand over his nearest one, and he flinched minutely as if he'd been unaware of her presence. When Lucy looked up at his face it was unbearably harsh, and she knew instantly that this man was worlds apart from the one-dimensional playboy tycoon she'd first believed him to be.

She didn't say anything, just kept her hand on his, and after a long moment he said, so quietly that she had to strain to hear, 'I remember being here…in this house…with my mother and father on holiday, just before she died. Ya-ya was still alive too, and my aunt…and we were happy. Really happy.'

Lucy didn't interrupt.

'My father had met my mother when he'd come here on a day-trip with some friends. They were typical Athenians— cocky, arrogant, rich… But he saw her, and within a month he'd taken her back to Athens to be his wife.'

'He must have loved her a great deal.'

Ari jerked his head to look down at Lucy. She felt tension spike in his form as if he'd just realised that he'd spoken out loud and had a witness.

'Loved her so much that after she died he married again within the year? *Please.* My father left me here with my grandmother, and the next time I remember seeing him he had Helen Savakis with him. His new wife.' His lip curled. 'She convinced him to send me to boarding school, where I was conveniently out of the way, so that she could have her own son and raise him to be my father's golden child.'

Lucy's shock at Helen's cold-hearted ruthlessness was palpable. 'But your father left everything to you…?'

Ari nodded, looking back out to sea. 'Which is why Anatolios hates me and Helen despises me even more now than she did when I was a child. She hates the fact that she needs me for her security. She hates the fact that I'm not in Athens, where she can try to make me marry a woman of her choosing to control me even more…'

Lucy winced reflexively at his mention of marriage and remembered his caustic response to Helen's obvious fear that what was between *them* might be serious. She guessed in that moment that Ari's memory of this place and that time when his parents were together ran deep for a reason. If they'd had a halcyon time here, only for his mother to die so suddenly and his father disappear, it must have been heartbreakingly confusing for a small child. How would someone so tiny make any sense of loving a place when it was also the scene of such sorrow?

But from the sounds of it, if his father had been a successful young man, with the world at his feet, it must have been love for him to marry Ari's mother, who would have been very poor.

'I can only imagine how hard it must have been for your father to leave you behind...perhaps that's why he married again so soon...'

Ari turned then, and looked down at Lucy properly. She felt very exposed in the face of his deep hurt and unmistakable cynicism.

'Yes—and why he found it no chore to send me away to school on his new wife's recommendation.'

'Ari, I've seen the way a woman can enchant a man. Maybe he was just—'

Just enchanted the way you're being enchanted right now? The revelation made Ari's voice harsh. 'What, Lucy? Please don't try and feed me some psychobabble nonsense. This subject is closed for discussion.' His eyes flashed a warning in the silvery light. 'And you're far too overdressed.'

Ari picked Lucy up with an intensity that sent a flutter of fear through her. Instinctively her hands tightened on his shoulders. And then something happened. Almost instantaneously she sensed a different intensity run through him. The mood altered. He looked down at her and she could see feral desire mixed with something almost like confusion in those dark green depths, and her heart ached with a mirror emotion.

The fact that she could sense his need to dilute the emotion he'd just revealed with physicality made her reach up and touch her mouth to his. She felt him tremble slightly, and as she wrapped her arms around his neck and deepened the kiss he responded.

He took her over to the bed and laid her down with a gentleness Lucy would have bet he hadn't been feeling just moments ago. The fact that she was so aware of him, aware of what was going on inside his head, made her reel anew. His body covered hers with a delicious weight and Lucy brought a shaky hand to his face. When he turned to press a kiss to her inner palm she felt another flutter of fear—but this time it was because she knew for certain that she'd fallen in love with this complex, proud man who presented one face to the world and another here with her.

When Lucy woke the next morning she wasn't surprised to see Ari up and dressed and sitting on the balcony. Dark glasses shielded those amazing eyes. There was a stillness to his body and a sternness to his features that told her the sensual cocoon they'd inhabited last night was gone. The revelation of admitting she'd fallen for him made her feel intensely vulnerable in the harsh light of day. She pulled the sheet up over her body and Ari's head turned. Her skin prickled when she imagined the slow appraisal he was giving her from behind those shades.

She came up on one arm and pushed her heavy mass of hair back, feeling very rumpled and lethargic. Ari had been ruthless in his pursuit of pleasure last night, *hers and his,* surprising her with the depth of passion he'd incited within her. It had seemed as if their lovemaking had gone to another place, and Lucy cringed inwardly now to remember that she'd been moved to tears after one shattering climax after another.

Now Ari just uncoiled that long lean body from the chair and said coolly, 'We need to get back to Athens. We've got work to do and a heavy week coming up.'

Lucy felt as if he'd slapped her. Her body went cold. Boss/assistant. Back to work. Back in her place. The intense vulnerability made her feel slightly sick.

'Of course,' she said through numb lips, when she felt like saying something like, *I never asked for this, you know, and I certainly never expected to be brought here to this idyllic little hideaway where you couldn't contain your emotions.*

When Lucy stood under the shower a short time later her belly clenched painfully. She could see exactly why he'd brought her here now: no possibility of paparazzi catching them out, no one who knew him apart from the locals he'd known as a child…*no chance for her to be getting any ideas.*

There was a knock on the door that made her jump, and Lucy heard a curt, 'The helicopter is on stand-by. As soon as you're ready we're leaving.'

'Fine,' Lucy called casually, belying the unsteady beating of her heart and the sick feeling gripping her gut. His words and cool manner were an all too mocking confirmation of her fears and her own stupidity. He was hustling them out of here as if there had just been some kind of dire weather warning, making it patently obvious how much he regretted bringing her there in the first place.

As she switched off the shower and stepped out, she knew that she would have to start distancing herself. She couldn't go on like this. She was being served a timely reminder of what she could expect out of this relationship—which was nothing but a very bruised heart.

That evening, when they returned to the hotel from Ari's Athens office and Lucy felt Ari take her arm as they stepped out of the lift, she drew on all her strength to pull away from his touch.

They approached her hotel room door and she prayed silently that he wouldn't try to come in. She sent him a quick glance, while swiping her door open at the same time, thanking God that her hands were steady.

'I'm tired. I'm going to go to bed…'

Her door opened and she heard a drawling, 'Not a bad idea.'

Lucy turned in the door and looked up. '*Alone*. As you said yourself earlier, we have a heavy week. And I—I am tired.'

Ari looked down at Lucy and felt the knot of frustration which had started the minute he'd left their bed earlier this morning intensify. Every moment he spent not touching this woman meant dealing with a level of frustration he hadn't experienced before. He looked at her properly for the first time. He'd tried to avoid looking directly at her all day—if he was honest since last night, when she'd— His belly flipped over and he ruthlessly quashed the memory of such weakness. He still couldn't believe it had happened…

But now she did look tired, with faint circles of violet under her eyes. She also looked a little strained, and a dart of guilt struck him when he remembered the urgency he'd felt to get off Paros and back here, bringing them straight to the office and working them both like dogs.

Lust was a force within him, crying out for satisfaction…but he would not admit to that. She wanted to go to bed alone? Well, he was damned if he was going to let her see that the notion of that went against every clamouring instinct to throw her over his shoulder and carry her to his own bed.

So he backed away, and did not like the visible look of relief that crossed her face. He almost stopped and gave in to his primal urges—had to clench his fists not to.

'We leave for Parnassus' villa at nine a.m. I'll see you in the lobby.'

She nodded and then disappeared into her room, shutting the door between them with a firm click that seemed to resonate all the way through Ari's body right to his feet.

On Thursday evening Lucy thought back to the gentle exhaustion she'd felt the previous Sunday and could have laughed. Since then it had been like the first week—a frenetic blur of work, whizzing from Parnassus' villa, back to Ari's office, and back to the hotel. Ari had been out late nearly every evening, having private meetings with Parnassus and their legal teams, and much to Lucy's relief hadn't thought it necessary for her to be there too.

She'd carefully locked the interconnecting door on her side each night, even though all she'd fantasised about was slipping naked between Ari's sheets and awaiting his return.

Instead, as she'd thumped her pillow, she'd told herself that this was the best way. Nip it in the bud now, and when they got back to the UK she'd calmly inform him that this brief moment of madness was over. Her mind froze at the thought of calling women for him, arranging dates, seeing him come in in the morning with that satisfied look on his face, slight shadows under those amazing eyes from not sleeping—

'Lucy, what are you doing hiding over here? Has Ari told you to stay out of sight in case people realise he's sleeping with his PA?'

It took a moment for Lucy's focus to return to the room and realise that Anatolios was standing in front of her, with a smarmy look on his face. She could almost feel sorry for him now that she knew he'd been rejected in the end, despite his mother's vast efforts to secure him number one place in his father's affections.

'I'm not hiding.' She felt defensive. She *had* been guilty

of hiding, hoping to get a glimpse of Ari and compose herself before going over to him. 'I've just arrived and I was looking for Ari.'

They'd come separately to this, another charity ball which was being held in their hotel in honour of Parnassus' contribution to helping the homeless in Athens. It was going to be the precursor of the announcement of the merger, which would be made the following morning, with the papers being signed at a press conference.

Lucy felt a prickle of unease skate up her spine when she saw how Anatolios's eyes were all but devouring her breasts, and she realised she was hemmed in between him and a wall. She moved to try and edge past him, but he moved too, surprising her with his agility.

He came and stood close, effectively blocking her from the room, and Lucy was very aware of how intimate it might look. She was plastered against the wall behind her now, could feel Anatolios's breath, smell the alcohol. Her belly spasmed.

'Anatolios, I have to go and find Ari. Would you excuse me, please?'

He laughed, and it was nasty. He didn't move. 'You English, you're always so polite—please and thank you. You're not going anywhere until you tell me what Ari is cooking up with Parnassus.'

Lucy flushed, and her eyes were immediately caught by Anatolios's. He couldn't hide his look of triumph.

'I *knew* it. I knew there was something big going on.' He grabbed Lucy's arm then, making her wince.

'Tell me what it is *right now*, I have a right to know what my brother is—'

Abruptly Anatolios was moved out of the way bodily, and then Ari was standing there. Lucy felt weak with relief.

He gestured with a hand for her to come with him, and she went gratefully, her legs feeling like jelly. She didn't look back, and when Ari said to her, 'What was going on there?' she avoided his eye and shook her head, saying, 'Nothing. He just…we were just chatting, that's all.'

The whole scene, with its air of menace, was making her feel sick, but she didn't see the point in rising Ari's ire now, when the deal was all but done.

Lucy made sure to stick close to him after that, figuring the devil she knew was better than dealing with Anatolios or Helen, who she'd also seen in the distance.

Just before everyone started to disperse Ari pulled her aside and took a sheaf of folded documents out of his inside jacket pocket. He handed them to her and they were still warm from his body heat. Even that made her tremble.

'Put these up in the safe in my room, would you, please? They're the official merger documents for tomorrow.'

She just nodded, avoiding his eye, and hurried out of the ballroom, glad of the respite and a chance to get herself back under control.

Ari watched Lucy leave the room, his eyes drawn helplessly to her glorious body in the figure-hugging strapless dress. His hunger for her was like a wild thing within him— a beast clawing to get out.

He rationalised it: it had to be because she'd been holding him at arm's length all week, her door firmly closed by the time he'd come back each evening. His mind had been helplessly distracted, despite the fact that he'd told her *not* to come to those late-night meetings, but now— His body tightened unbearably. The thought of her right now, in his room… He glanced around and knew he wouldn't be missed for a few moments. His blood surged at the thought of tumbling her onto his bed and sating this demon desire inside him.

* * *

Lucy was walking over to where the safe was hidden in the wardrobe of Ari's bedroom when she heard something at the door. She turned and went back, thinking it might be the turn down staff. When she saw Anatolios slipping into the room she froze.

'What are you doing here? How did you get in?'

He smiled nastily, and she saw his eyes take in the documents in her hand. She hurriedly put them behind her back.

He kept coming towards her, and she started to back away into the bedroom.

'Oh, let's just say I'm in Athens a lot more than Ari these days, so I have my contacts. Now, why don't you show me what you have hidden behind your pretty back?'

He was coming straight at her and Lucy froze for a second, fear gripping her like a cold, clammy hand. He was almost on her before she turned and stumbled, making for the safe before he could get the documents from her.

She felt her arm grabbed in a merciless grip and cried out, tipping off balance. Anatolios jerked her back painfully.

'Let me *go*.'

He was reaching around her, trying to get the papers, his face red and flushed. In a bid to get away, though his arms were wrapped tight around her now, Lucy dropped the papers behind her and used her hands to try and push him off. He saw the papers and lunged, knocking them both to the ground. He fell as a heavy weight on top of her, reaching underneath her for the papers.

Lucy was struggling in earnest now. She could feel her dress riding up her leg, her chest being squashed by his heavy weight. 'You... Get off me. I can't...*breathe*...'

'What the hell is going on here?'

CHAPTER NINE

BEFORE Lucy knew which way was up, the heavy weight of Anatolios was being plucked off her by Ari, as if he weighed no more than a bag of sugar. He literally held Anatolios by the scruff of his neck. The man was spluttering now, clearly terrified of his much stronger older brother.

'She told me to come up here. She told me she had something for me. *There!*'

He pointed to the papers, now strewn on the ground.

'Is this true?' Icy green eyes and an even icier voice were directed down at Lucy, who realised that she was still on the floor, dress hitched up, breasts heaving with her breath. She scrambled up, but then had to subside onto the side of the bed when her legs wouldn't hold her. Reaction was starting to set in.

She shook her head. She couldn't look at Ari—or *him*. 'No, of course it's not true. He followed me up here. He must have seen you give me the papers.'

Anatolios spluttered even more. 'Come *on*. Why on earth would I want to see some stupid papers? It's not as if there's anything going on—is there?'

Ari stilled. Right until that moment his vision had been blurred because he was so angry. When he'd seen Anatolios on top of Lucy he'd felt an awful weakness pervade his limbs before he'd kicked into action. And then, when he'd seen the papers… His heart was telling him one thing, but his brain was refusing to listen.

He dragged Anatolios to the door of the suite and said blisteringly, 'If I find out that you were the instigator of this incident you can kiss goodbye to working for Levakis Enterprises once and for all.'

And with that he threw his brother out of the suite and faced back to the bedroom, thinking to himself, *If, on the other hand, I find out it was Lucy…* His brain seized.

She appeared at the bedroom door. She looked unsteady on her feet, one shoe on, one shoe off. Her dark hair was tumbled in glorious profusion around her milky pale bare shoulders, the curve of her breasts outlined by the top of her strapless dress. As if seeing the direction of his gaze, she put her hands there and hitched the dress up. He noticed they were shaking, and yet he couldn't give in to his overwhelming instinct which was to go to her, to take her into his arms. He *couldn't*—because she might very well have just tried to betray him in the most heinous way.

He suddenly thought of the way he'd seen her earlier, backed into a corner talking to Anatolios as intimately as if they'd been lovers. And thought too of all the distant warning bells he'd ignored in his pursuit of her. The fact that work had taken second place, especially at such an important time, was starkly clear now.

Lucy sucked in a sharp breath. Ari clearly wasn't leaping to see if she was all right as he stood there, all but glowering at her. The fact that he believed she *might* have led Anatolios up here with a view to giving him or showing him the documents was screamingly obvious. Her hand gripped onto the doorframe as sheer hurt at his fundamental lack of trust nearly floored her.

He moved suddenly, and she flinched, but he just went over

to the drinks board and poured a measure of what looked like whisky into a shot glass and brought it over to her.

'Here—drink this.'

She looked up as she took the glass. 'Ari, please let me—'

'I don't want to hear it. Not right now anyway.'

And he stepped past her and into the room, where she looked back to see him pick up the papers and put them in the safe.

Feeling numb, Lucy bent to take off her one shoe and went into the sitting room to sit down. She took a sip of the liquid, wincing as it burnt its way down her throat.

Ari came back out and stood with arms folded, all but towering over her. She refused to cower back into the chair, and put the glass down jerkily on the table beside her.

'Ari—'

'Did he see the papers? Does he know about Parnassus?'

'Of course not. How can you think that?'

'Because tonight is the second time I've seen you deep in conversation with my brother, and now, the night before the biggest merger in Greek history is announced, he happens to be conveniently in the same room as you when you're putting the papers in the safe.' His mouth thinned. 'Although obviously you both got distracted—'

Lucy stood, quivering from head to toe. 'Stop that right now. That's not how it happened. He followed me up here and got in somehow. He must have got a key from someone on the staff. Before I knew it he was…' She shuddered convulsively as she remembered the instant panic at feeling him crowding her, all over her.

Lucy stopped talking and looked into those devastating and yet icy green eyes, that harsh face. Her words might as well have been addressed to a marble statue. He was so remote, so *untouchable*. And something slammed into her consciousness. It was cold and stark reality. Despite his cool behaviour that last morning on Paros, had she really fooled herself for a second into believing that something amazing had happened between them? That against all the odds they'd gained some sort of mutual trust and respect? She was just the secretary and he was her boss… She gasped audibly as it became even more clear, her hand going to her chest as if to stop the lancing pain. But it didn't.

Even Ari frowned. 'What is it?'

Lucy figured dimly that all the colour must have drained from her face. She felt icy cold all of a sudden, and tried to formulate words through numb lips. 'That's why you appeared—you didn't even trust me to come up here and do this. You suspected something all along.'

She watched as his face flushed a dark red, and found herself sinking back down onto the chair.

'All this time you've thought that I might do something like this.' She shook her head and looked up, pain shattering her insides as she had to ask, 'Is that why you slept with me? Because you thought it might be easier to control me?'

His lack of response and that stony visage was confirmation enough. As if watching a movie in slow motion, Lucy went all the way back to when she'd tried to resign and Ari had told her she couldn't. It must have been then. He must have decided at that point that she might be a liability and planning some kind of revenge.

She somehow found the strength to stand again. She felt even clammier now. She'd always known what Ari was, the kind of man he was, but somehow in the past few weeks she'd let herself forget it.

He put out a hand towards her but Lucy flinched back, moving behind the chair,

'Lucy—'

'*No*. I don't want to hear it. I know it's over. It's all over. That's the only reason you slept with me. I've been really—'

She stopped and bit her lip before she could say *stupid*. She lifted dead eyes to his. 'Blood really is thicker than water, isn't it?' She smiled a small harsh smile. 'Perhaps this is a step forward in fostering a new regard for your half-brother?'

Her smile faded. 'Anatolios doesn't know about the merger. It happened exactly the way I said it did. The reason I passed off the conversation earlier as nothing was because he was beginning to suspect something and asked me about it. I didn't tell you because I figured he'd never find out before the morning and you didn't need the hassle.'

She hitched up her chin. 'I intend to resign once the press conference is over, I can't see why you wouldn't agree to that now.' She smiled with brittle brightness. 'After all, I can't imagine you want to be faced with an assistant you had to sleep with for business every day.'

Lucy turned and walked stiffly to the door, then looked back, somewhere in his general direction. 'I can organise my own flight home tomorrow after the press conference. I'd prefer that, and I'm sure you would too. I'll work out my notice if you insist, but I'm happy to collect my things from the office on Monday too.'

And, opening the door, she slipped out.

Ari watched the door for a long moment. The earth was shifting underneath him. He *had* been about to refute her reasoning behind why he'd slept with her, but then, when she'd interrupted him and obviously decided that that had to be the case, he hadn't spoken up.

He could have stopped her from leaving. He could have told her. *Why* hadn't he?

Ari sat down heavily onto the ornately brocaded sofa behind him. Without the awful stomach-churning red mist of anger that had gripped him, he had to concede that of course he trusted Lucy over his opportunistic brother any day of the week. This whole scene had all the clumsy and unoriginal hallmarks of Anatolios. But he'd just seen them together and…his mind had imploded.

His fists clenched when he saw how easily he'd misinterpreted the situation. She was wrong in this case. Blood was most certainly not thicker than water. If Lucy had been guilty she'd never have jumped to the conclusion she had. She'd have defended herself vociferously, she'd have cajoled and enticed, perhaps even tried to seduce him into bed to distract him. But he didn't need reminding that she hadn't come near him since Paros. His mouth twisted. And could he blame her? When he'd all but hustled her off the island like a fugitive. But he had just been so…so overwhelmed that she'd witnessed his excruciating weakness. *She'd seen him cry.* And she hadn't turned away in horror, she'd been gorgeous, sympathetic, understanding… It had been too much.

He couldn't deal with that. No one had seen that side of him. It had been locked away for so long—he'd been alone against the world for so long…

And that was why he'd let her stand there and believe he'd seduced her deliberately. His life hadn't been on an even keel since he'd started noticing her, desiring her. That had been part of his knee-jerk response tonight—the knowledge that he'd been so hungry for her that he'd followed her to the room for *that* and not because he might have suspected her of espionage. He'd felt intensely vulnerable for the brief moment when he had contemplated that that could have been the reality.

He stood abruptly and made for the door. He had to go back downstairs, had to smile and pretend everything was OK, when he felt as if his insides were twisting tight in his gut. Lucy was right. It was over. Where could it go from here anyway? He would not let her see him be weak one more time. No woman was worth that.

* * *

The next morning, when the press conference was over, Lucy avoided the scrum of shocked and chattering press and went up to her room. She picked up her one small bag, she was leaving all the bought clothes behind, and went down to the lobby to check out.

She was just arranging for a taxi to take her to the airport when she felt her arm taken in a spine-tinglingly familiar grip and a smooth voice spoke over her to the concierge. 'My driver will look after her, thank you.'

She stiffened under his touch, her whole body crying out shamefully for more.

'That's really not necessary.'

He smoothly moved them away, his hand still on her arm. Lucy fought not to pull it free, afraid he might guess how badly he was affecting her.

'Lucy—' he sighed heavily '—about last night—'

'Please. You don't have to say anything.'

'I do.' His hand tightened, and she looked up against her better judgement. His eyes were so green that she felt pole-axed.

'You were wrong, I never slept with you because I thought you were capable of espionage. I read the situation entirely wrong and I'm sorry. But you're right…it's…this—*us*—is over.'

Lucy tried to school her features, even though she felt as if someone had just stabbed her in the belly. Relief that he *had* trusted her was eclipsed by sheer pain that she shouldn't even be feeling. 'What about…your brother?'

Ari grimaced. 'I'll deal with him. It's not for you to worry about.'

No, thought Lucy faintly, still reeling and hating herself for it. Because she wouldn't be working for Levakis Enterprises any more.

'Look, I'm leaving for New York from here for about ten

days, to make sure the merger goes smoothly over there. If you still intend to resign—'

For a second Lucy heard nothing but a roaring in her ears— *what other option did she possibly have?* It cleared just in time for her to hear him say, 'That should give you time to sort yourself out.'

Lucy nodded dumbly. Even though she *wanted* this, had asked for this, to be faced with it now was like no other devastation she'd ever felt. But how on earth had she thought it might play out? she admonished herself. Aristotle Levakis would never keep a discarded lover hanging around like a bad smell. And of course they couldn't go back to a benign working relationship, no matter how she'd thought it might happen.

Ari walked her out to the entrance, where his car was waiting. He handed her in and said, 'I want to thank you for all your work. This merger wouldn't have happened nearly as smoothly without you.'

Oh, please just don't, she almost said. Their affair was reduced to this—trite thanks for her work on the project and for pleasuring her boss in bed in between meetings. The glaring cliché of it all nearly made her want to be ill. Before she could lose control, Lucy grabbed the door handle and pulled it closed firmly, shutting Ari out, but not unfortunately, the pain.

She didn't look back as the car pulled away, so she didn't see Ari standing there, his features drawn and almost grey in the glorious Athenian sun. And anyway, even if she had she wouldn't have believed it.

It was Friday evening, a week later, and Lucy was packing her final bits and pieces into a box, looking around the now empty office. It had been infinitely easier to do this without Ari here, though it had been heart-wrenchingly painful to talk to him on the phone every day, when he'd called to check in or give instructions and hear how interviews were going for a new assistant.

'I trust you. After all, you've been the best assistant I've had,' he'd said when she'd protested that she couldn't be responsible for hiring someone new.

He'd made no effort to ask her to stay, and even though Lucy didn't even want that, couldn't contemplate that, she'd found it nauseating to shake the hand of the best candidate just the other day and had forced a brittle smile when the girl had said, 'Is it true what they say? Is he really that astoundingly gorgeous?'

Lucy shook her head now, to try and clear it, and pulled on her beige trenchcoat. She'd dressed down today, not having seen the point in making an effort, and was wearing jeans, an oversized black jumper and battered sneakers. Her thoughts in that moment went guiltily to her mum, and she bit her lip as she hefted up the box. She had to find another job, and soon. She'd be OK for the next few months or so, but after that—

'*Lucy.*'

Lucy whirled around at the familiar deep voice. It tugged on her insides and made a fire of sensation race across her skin. Her movement had been so sudden that the full box wobbled precariously out of her arms and fell to the floor, upending everything in a big mess.

She barely registered Ari standing at the door like a huge, dark and threatening presence, and bent down to start picking the things up, her hands shaking. He moved fast and crouched down. Lucy put out a hand. 'Please—don't. I can do it.'

But he ignored her, picking up books and stationery, putting things back in the box. Lucy had to break the taut silence. 'I thought you weren't coming back till the weekend.'

Had he been wining and dining some new woman already in New York? She slammed a book more furiously than she'd intended into the box, in reaction to her wayward thoughts and the jealousy that spiked through her gut.

Ari didn't seem to notice, calmly packing the box. His scent reached out and wrapped her in a heat haze of lust.

'I wrapped things up early. I wanted to get back here.'

His voice was cool, devoid of emotion.

Lucy's movements became brisker. She just wanted to get out of here—right now. 'I think you'll like Gemma, your new assistant. She was far and away the most qualified person.'

Everything was back in the box, and there was an awkward moment when Lucy and Ari went to pick it up at the same time. Lucy had to let him take it, or it would have fallen again.

'I thought I told you I don't like your hair tied back.'

Lucy's eyes flew to his in shock. He sounded almost *flirty*. And his eyes were dark, glittering in a way she hadn't seen since— Once again she cursed her fevered brain. 'That's hardly relevant any more.' She took the box firmly out of his hands and held it to her like a shield. She stepped neatly around him, her breathing feeling short and jerky. 'Well, I'd better—'

'You haven't found a new job yet, have you?'

Lucy turned around. When would this torture end? She longed to be able to say yes, feeling inherently ashamed that she hadn't found a job, as if it made her look unemployable. But every single company she'd approached had stone-walled her—hadn't even allowed her an interview. She couldn't understand it. With a glowing reference from Ari himself, she'd have thought it would be at least easier than it had.

She shook her head and could feel her low ponytail move as she did so. 'Not yet.' She lifted her chin. 'But I'm sure I will, sooner or later.'

Ari sat back on the edge of her desk and fire raced into Lucy's cheeks as she remembered one day in his office in

Athens, when he'd perched her on the edge of his desk, spread her legs and— She nearly dropped the box again.

'Look, I have to get going. I have to visit my mother.'

'How is she?'

Lucy wanted to scream. What was this? Twenty questions?

Her throat felt constricted. 'She's fine…well, as fine as she can be. She's comfortable—that's the main thing.'

Ari stood up then, hands in pockets. 'Lucy, I want to offer you another job here in the company. You don't have to work for me, you can work for the legal team again. A position has become vacant.'

She shook her head immediately, panic gripping her at the thought of not being able to escape from this man's devastating orbit. 'No, I don't want— That is, I'd prefer to seek employment elsewhere.'

He said nothing for a long, ominous moment, and then said quietly, 'You might find that more difficult than you think.'

Sick realisation sank in. The box slipped precariously in Lucy's arms but she gripped it tight. She thought of all the jobs she'd gone for in the past few days. The dead ends when she'd known that they were seeking people yet had turned her away.

'Did you—have you stopped me from getting jobs?'

Ari's jaw clenched. He didn't have to answer—he saw the dawning realisation on Lucy's face. 'I've changed my mind. I want you to stay here with Levakis Enterprises.'

His jaw clenched even harder. He'd changed his mind as soon as he'd seen his car pull away with her in it that day in Athens. 'I want to see you again, but I know it can't happen if you're my assistant. It wouldn't be fair on you. But this way it'll be much more acceptable.'

Shock, horror, *heat*—a complete mix of emotions rushed through Lucy with such force that she nearly fainted. She saw black spots before her eyes, but through them she saw Ari—

tall and proud and hard and implacable. And as ruthless as ever. Because he hadn't finished with her. *Yet.*

'You've changed your mind, you say? Well, I'm sorry,' she bit out, 'but I'm not available for the position of convenient mistress.'

He stood straighter, his face flushing. 'It doesn't have to be like that, Lucy. I'm asking you to be my lover. We were good together. I can't get you out of my mind...'

She shifted the box. Her arms were starting to ache. But when Ari saw the movement and made as if to take it out of her arms she jerked away. *'No.'*

This moment was so important to her—how she acted right now. Because if she followed the craving call of her body to give in she would be going the way of the doomed, of her mother. She would have learnt nothing. Her heart was bound up inextricably with this man, and he would crush it completely.

She felt a deep sadness well within her that she'd fallen for someone who could never love her as she now knew she ached to be loved. She ached to find the fulfilment she'd never seen as a child. To have the security that came from being in a committed, equal and loving relationship. The kind of thing she'd seen in Kallie and Alexandros Kouros.

'I don't want that, Ari. I don't want you...not like that. I'm worth more than a sleazy work affair, and, no matter how you try and pretty it up, that's all it would be.'

'There is another option. You don't have to work here. It could be much easier than that. I could show you the best that this world has to offer, take care of you and your mother—'

Lucy felt bile rise. She shook her head vehemently, her ponytail slipping over one shoulder. 'I won't be set up like that. I grew up with that, and it's something I just won't settle for. I can look after myself and my mother just fine. We don't need you or any other man.'

Lucy saw Ari's fists clench at his sides at her rejection of his offer. His voice had a rough quality that somehow jarred with his autocratic behaviour, but Lucy didn't have time to dwell on the meaning of that. 'Well, good luck finding a job, Lucy…I'll be waiting for your call when you realise you won't get one. I've marked you as exclusive to this company—no one will touch you with a bargepole.'

Lucy felt tears prick the backs of her eyes when she thought of what a precarious position that would put her mother in. '*Why* are you insisting on doing this?'

He said something guttural in Greek, his face unbearably harsh. 'I told you. I want you. This isn't over between us. I'll expect you to be in Theo's office on Monday morning. I know you can't move from London without jeopardising your mother's treatment.'

Right then Lucy hated Ari, and yet even as she thought that her heart clenched—because she knew she didn't. She couldn't. She tried to make her voice sound as cool and calm as possible, and prayed that for once her every emotion wasn't showing on her too-expressive face.

'I will not be manipulated like this, and I *won't* be falling back into your bed. You'd have to knock me out and drag me there like the neanderthal you're behaving like now.'

His face flushed again, but she didn't mistake the glint of triumph, despite her petty barb. He thought he had her right where he wanted her, but Lucy vowed not to succumb—no matter what he might try or what he was threatening. She turned and stalked from the room, realising that she'd never see him again, at least not in person, and the pain that ripped through her nearly made her stumble and fall.

It was only his softly spoken mocking words that came from behind her that helped her to keep going.

'See you on Monday morning, Lucy.'

CHAPTER TEN

ON MONDAY morning Ari strode authoritatively through his own building. The gasps and shocked murmurs as he passed people by merely bounced off him. Aristotle Levakis never frequented any office or floor of the building but his own. His blood was humming, anticipation a taut wire of need, and all because he was going to see Lucy any second now—and because seeing her the other day after a week's absence had shown him that even one day was too long. He vowed there and then to make sure it didn't happen again.

He was too far gone to try and deny the fact that she had him wound so tight around her little finger that he couldn't think straight. For the entire weekend his conscience had been pricking him but he'd quashed it down with a strength of will that was matched only by the strength of his desire for this woman. As he walked towards her office he finally had to acknowledge that he felt out of control for the first time in his life. One thought and one thought only had dominated since he'd seen her last: he wanted her, he needed her, and anything was better than her leaving—

He stopped in his tracks when he pushed open the outer door to his legal team's offices only to see an empty chair where Lucy should have been sitting—*where the hell was she?*

The immediate hollow ache in his solar plexus stunned him

with its force. Just then Theo strolled out of his office, a frown on his face.

'Ari? What's up?'

What's up? Ari felt dizzy for a second. He bit out, 'Lucy Proctor—where is she?'

He was hardly aware of Theo's frown and obvious confusion. 'I thought you knew…? She rang this morning and said she wouldn't be taking the position—said something about wanting some time off. I won't lie, I was delighted when you said she was going to be back working for us, but now…'

Ari didn't hear the rest of whatever Theo said. He left. When he got back up to his office he shut the door on his new PA's concerned face and found that he was shaking. Actually shaking. Aristotle Levakis—shaking like a leaf.

With a roaring in his ears he went over to his drinks cabinet and poured himself a drink. He downed it in one. For the first time in his life he did not know what to do. He sat down heavily in his chair and stared vacantly into the distance.

She'd gone. She'd not been playing coy. He'd not backed her into a corner with his threats to derail her chances of getting work. And, if anything, to remember what he'd done and said, the lengths he'd gone to to keep her near, made him feel ill. Especially when he thought of her mother and how much it meant to Lucy to have her taken care of. Immediately he went to reach for the phone, to call her and tell her that everything would be fine, that he'd look after her mother. He stopped.

He'd already done that. He'd already offered her his protection, the exalted position of his mistress, and she'd turned him down. Again bile rose as he realised he'd offered her the one thing she'd refuse even if her life depended on it. Ari sat back and closed his eyes, something awful like dread trickling through him, gathering force as it did so.

* * *

Lucy felt as brittle as a Chinese Ming vase teetering on the edge of a table. It had been two weeks since she'd *not* walked back into Levakis Enterprises to take the job that had been so ungraciously offered to her. She still felt sick to her belly to know that despite everything, despite all she'd shared with Ari of her life, he'd turned around and offered to *take care of her*.

And yet as she sat here now in her mother's bedroom, holding the book she'd been reading from aloud, she missed him with an ache that seemed to be growing more acute and stronger by the minute. She was constantly bombarded with images of their time together, and, worse, she'd even caught herself in a daydream of them together, *with a family*, before she could stop herself. Having never believed she was the slightest bit maternal, it was as if she'd suddenly tapped into some universal compulsion to have a baby. With him.

Her mother shifted restlessly and Lucy looked at her, smoothing some hair off her brow. She'd fallen asleep as Lucy had read to her.

Lucy hadn't had the heart to fight the uphill battle to look for a new job yet, so she'd spent the last two weeks coming to see her mum every day, but time was running out. She needed to get work fast. Her mouth firmed as the familiar pain rose. More than that, she needed to forget about—

'Lucy, love, someone here to see you.'

Lucy looked up and blushed. She'd been so caught up in her thoughts she hadn't heard the woman come in. She stood up, and as she followed the nurse out she wondered who on earth it could be…here of all places.

When she came out into the corridor the world swirled crazily. So crazily that she must have swayed, because before she knew it Ari was in front of her and holding onto her, looking down into her eyes.

With a deep inner cry of dismay Lucy wondered if she was

conjuring him up, and if it was in fact just her mother's consultant. She blinked. Ari. She blinked again. *Ari.*

From somewhere deeply welcome she came back to earth and pulled herself free of his touch. She stalked to a small empty waiting area nearby. She crossed her arms and turned around, feeling her cheeks grow hot as she took in the reality of facing him again. Those recent images of small dark-haired babies mocked her.

'What are you doing here?' She injected all the frost she could muster into her voice, but when Ari winced imperceptibly she treacherously felt nothing but remorse.

He looked awful. As if he hadn't slept in a week or shaved in days. He was wearing jeans and a sweater, nothing like the cool urbane businessman she'd first seen at a distance two years ago. He was more like the man she'd seen on Paros. Her heart clenched painfully.

He looked at her, and she quailed inwardly but tipped up her chin. When he spoke she had to strain to listen.

'I thought that here might be the only place you'd speak to me. Please forgive me for intruding on your personal space with your mother.'

One fire died in Lucy's belly and another started. Her arms relaxed fractionally. How was it that he still had the power to surprise her, damn him?

'Lucy, I want you to come back to Greece with me. Right now. I want to show you something. I need to talk to you but I can't…' He looked around for a moment. 'Not here…'

Lucy's arms tightened again. She shook her head fiercely. *Go back to Greece?* He had to be kidding. The thought of being in close proximity to this man was about as dangerous as sky-diving without a parachute.

He registered her reaction and Lucy saw something flicker in his eyes.

'Lucy, *please.*'

Something in the quality of his voice made her stop, but still she shook her head. Nothing on this earth would persuade her to set herself up to be hurt again. She crushed the treacherous need to know answers: why did he want her to go to Greece? Why wasn't he sweeping in here and demanding to know why she hadn't taken the job? It was what she might have expected. Why wasn't he acting like the proud, arrogant man she knew? And—the worst question of all—why had it taken him two weeks to come after her?

Ari's jaw clenched and something trickled down Lucy's spine. She saw a glimpse of the man she knew. Hard and implacable.

'Very well, if the only way I can persuade you to come is by threatening to reveal to the press that your mother is here, then so be it.'

Lucy gasped and went icy cold. On some level she was certain that Ari would never do such a thing, but on another level she wasn't absolutely sure, and the fact that he was even threatening such a thing made her feel acutely disappointed, and if she was disappointed what did that say about her own pathetically skewed judgment?

'You absolute *bastard*.'

He stepped forward and she stepped back, seeing colour flash through his cheeks. He held out a hand imperiously, and when she didn't move he just dropped it and said, sounding utterly defeated, 'I don't know where that came from. I'm sorry. Of course I wouldn't do that to you or your mother. I just want you to come with me so that I can show you something and talk to you…I promise that if you want to return after you've seen it and we've talked, I'll bring you straight back here.'

Lucy looked at him for a long moment. She was already starting to drown in those green depths. The real and awful truth was that she'd go to the ends of the earth if this man asked her. A very weak part of her was saying, *Go, go, go,* and she could already feel resistance washing away. He was confusing her with his behaviour, with the vulnerability she'd glimpsed but couldn't quite believe. Even so, she had every intention of keeping him to his word.

She said tightly, 'You promise? Then you'll leave me alone and let me find another job?'

He nodded. 'I'll make sure nothing stands in your way.'

Lucy waited for what seemed like an interminable moment, and then finally said, 'I'll get my jacket and bag.'

A scant few hours later they were landing at Athens airport, and Lucy still felt slightly winded at knowing that she'd been sitting at her mother's bedside just hours before. The steward opened the plane door and Ari stood and held out a hand. Lucy looked at it. They hadn't spoken a word on the flight. Ari had been sternly cold.

Feeling intense trepidation, she put her hand in his and let him pull her up. He led her out, and then they were climbing into a nearby helicopter, which was lifting into the clear blue sky within minutes.

Lucy's hands were tightly clasped in her lap, and she avoided looking at Ari as much as possible. After a while Lucy could see that they were circling an island, and she recognised Paros. A mixture of sheer pleasure and intense pain gripped her. If he'd brought her here just to—

But the helicopter was landing, and then they were out, and it was just Lucy and Ari, standing by the same Jeep they'd used the last time. Memories were too intense.

Lucy backed away and mocked herself inwardly for having such a weak and delayed reaction. He'd got her here by barely saying please. She was pathetic.

'Ari, if we're just here so that you can—'

He came and stood close—too close. 'Lucy, please, just trust me. A little further, that's all.'

Where could she go anyway? Lucy looked around. They were miles from anything. Silently she got into the Jeep. Ari got in too, and then they were driving. When she recognised the signs for his mother's tiny village Ari turned and went eastwards. After another ten minutes he took a sharp left turn down towards the coast, and they stopped at a set of ancient wrought-iron gates, nearly overgrown with vegetation.

Ari came round to meet Lucy. He helped her out but when he saw her open her mouth as if to speak he put a finger to her lips. He'd never been so terrified in his entire life; his heart was hammering painfully.

'This is what I wanted to show you.'

The feel of her soft lips against his finger nearly undid him, but he controlled himself.

He led her in through the gate, which was hanging off its hinges, then down an overgrown path and out into a huge clearing where an old and rambling villa, clearly dilapidated, stood on a bluff overlooking the sea.

Lucy's hand tightened reflexively in Ari's. It must have been stunning in its heyday, and the view was priceless. Already she could imagine what it might be like if it was done up, restored to its former glory.

'What is this place?'

Ari brought her over to the other side of the house and an unimpeded view of the sea to where a trail led down to a private beach.

'I bought it…signed the papers just yesterday.'

Lucy felt a little bewildered. He'd brought her here to show her his latest acquisition? 'Oh…well, congratulations.'

He turned and looked at her intently. 'You like it, don't you?'

Lucy frowned, feeling very vulnerable. 'Well, of course I like it. It's beautiful, idyllic, but what does it matter what I think about it?'

He didn't say anything for a long moment, and then he said, 'Because I bought it for you…for us.'

Lucy tried to make sense of his words, feeling a little spaced-out. 'You mean…?' Something struck her then, and anger flowered deep down. She took her hand from his. 'Ari, if you've bought this as some kind of…of love-nest, just so that I can be your mistress—'

He was shaking his head, a curious light in his eyes. 'No. I want it to be a home—a place where we can come…perhaps even with a family…'

Lucy was starting to flounder badly. His words were making all sorts of things bloom in her heart, making it beat faster. How could he know of her deeply secret daydreams? It felt as if he was looking straight into her head. 'Ari—I don't… What are you talking about…?'

He brought a shaking hand to her face, his eyes so intense it nearly hurt to look at them. 'Lucy, I brought you here because *here* is the only place I know how to be me, where I can say what I need to say. I've been going crazy these past two weeks. At first I told myself I didn't need you, that I wasn't devastated beyond belief when I found out you hadn't taken the job with Theo. And then one night, at three o'clock in the morning, when I found myself driving to your flat and sitting outside like a stalker, I had to face up to myself.'

He took a deep breath. 'I think I fell in love with you when you appeared like a whirling dervish to defend me against Helen. I've never had anyone stand up for me before—*care about me before*. I've never *needed* it. But you made me realise how lonely I've been all my life.'

His mouth twisted. 'I thought I had it all figured out. I'd keep you on in the company if you insisted on working, but essentially I wanted you as my mistress. It was only when I said the words out loud I realised what an insult it was—especially to you, after all you've been through. And it was then that I knew I wanted much, much more than that. I wanted everything. A life together. *A marriage.*'

He laughed harshly. 'Of course I denied it to myself. *Love?* I'd cut myself off from anything like that when I was sent away to England and it became my home. Helen effectively cut me off from my father, wouldn't even allow a normal relationship to develop between me and my brother. That's why I'd locked away my memories of here and my mother…I couldn't believe it had existed. But meeting you, falling in love with you, made me believe in them again. It made me remember the love I felt.'

Lucy was more than shocked. She was in danger of floating away from her body. But at the same time she felt welded to the ground, incapable of processing his words, because she realised just how badly she wanted this. And yet…

'But I heard what you said to Helen just before she hit you…about never marrying someone like me…'

Ari looked confused for a moment, and then his face cleared. '*Thee mou*, that wasn't about *you*. Helen was suggesting I marry Pia Kyriapoulos, which would have suited her ends perfectly and kept me marginalized. Pia is not exactly the epitome of the blushing Greek bride.'

'Oh.' Lucy tried to look down, away from his intensity, but Ari wouldn't let her budge.

He took something out of his back pocket and held it out to Lucy. It was a small velvet bag. She looked at him and he just said, 'Open it—please…'

She was all fingers and thumbs, so Ari helped her, and then it was open and something fell into her hand. It was the stunning butterfly necklace she'd seen all those weeks ago and it glinted up at her now. She felt her eyes film over with tears. Ari took it and placed it tenderly around her neck, making tingles run up and down her spine. He tipped her chin up again, forcing her gaze to meet his. His eyes blazed into hers.

'So will you, Lucy Proctor—marry me? Please? Because I cannot imagine going forward from this day or this place without you by my side.'

Emotion was cracking open inside Lucy, and it was the most gloriously painful thing she'd ever felt in her life.

'I never wanted to feel this much.'

Ari's mouth quirked. 'It's painful, isn't it?'

It was the sudden complicit feeling of mutual emotion and how similar they really were in their hearts that made Lucy's eyes water in earnest. Her mouth wobbled precariously. 'I thought I'd settle for someone boring—someone who wouldn't make me face up to myself, to the desires I kept hidden. But you made me believe I had nothing to be scared of... I love you, Ari. I fell for you the day you gave that stupidly expensive necklace to two strangers in the street. And it was when you brought me here that I knew I'd fallen in love with you. And, yes, I'll marry you.'

Lucy could feel the tremor in his hands as they framed her face.

'Thank God,' he said huskily, and bent his head to seal their vow with barely restrained passion.

When they broke apart she could still feel his hands trembling, and his face had such an endearing mix of expressions—pure Ari arrogance and then something she'd never seen before, sheer childlike *joy*—that she couldn't help smiling at him.

He returned her gaze, and for just a moment Lucy caught a glimpse of something achingly vulnerable cross his face before he said haltingly, 'That night I was sitting outside your flat, apart from lurid fantasies featuring a certain tight skirt, I found myself imagining you pregnant...having a baby...*our* baby. I suddenly wanted a family. And not just for an heir...but to create something—a secure foundation. It scared me to death, and it's the only thing that's held me back from coming for you sooner.' He quirked an unsteady smile. 'That and the fact that you might reject me. But the thing is…I've no idea how you feel about kids…'

Lucy looked up at him and wondered how her heart hadn't exploded into tiny pieces. 'Funny you should mention that…'

In more or less exactly the same spot where Ari had proposed to her three years before, Lucy shaded her eyes and looked down to the private beach, where her husband was holding their son high in the air before dunking him back in the glittering sea. The childish shrieks of delight made her smile and she sat down, rearranging the tiny baby in her arms so that she could feed her from the other breast.

'You're very happy, darling, aren't you?'

Lucy looked over to her mother, who was sitting in a wheelchair in the shade on the other side of the table, and smiled. 'Yes, Mum…I am.' Her mother looked away again, out to sea, with an enigmatic smile of her own.

Maxine had these moments of lucidity every now and then, ever since Lucy and Ari had moved her here to the refurbished villa on Paros permanently, with a full-time nursing staff to take care of her every need. Her Alzheimer's hadn't improved, but it seemed to have slowed its development, and sometimes when Lucy looked at her she knew her mother was imagining herself to be in this beautiful place being cared for by one of her besotted suitors.

Lucy had insisted on Ari keeping his mother's house nearby exactly as it was, and sometimes they went back for a night on their own, and revelled in their private space that no one knew about.

Just then a dripping wet Ari appeared, holding an exuberant Cosmo steadily on his shoulders. He smiled widely, his eyes flashing with secret promise and something much deeper and more enduring—*love*. Lucy couldn't remember when she'd once wondered what he'd look like if he smiled. She smiled back, for life was good.

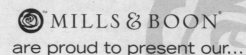

millsandboon.co.uk Community

Join Us!

The Community is the perfect place to meet and chat to kindred spirits who love books and reading as much as you do, but it's also the place to:

- Get the inside scoop from authors about their latest books
- Learn how to write a romance book with advice from our editors
- Help us to continue publishing the best in women's fiction
- Share your thoughts on the books we publish
- Befriend other users

Forums: Interact with each other as well as authors, editors and a whole host of other users worldwide.

Blogs: Every registered community member has their own blog to tell the world what they're up to and what's on their mind.

Book Challenge: We're aiming to read 5,000 books and have joined forces with The Reading Agency in our inaugural Book Challenge.

Profile Page: Showcase yourself and keep a record of your recent community activity.

Social Networking: We've added buttons at the end of every post to share via digg, Facebook, Google, Yahoo, technorati and de.licio.us.

www.millsandboon.co.uk

2 FREE BOOKS
AND A SURPRISE GIFT

We would like to take this opportunity to thank you for reading this Mills & Boon® book by offering you the chance to take TWO more specially selected books from the Modern™ series absolutely FREE! We're also making this offer to introduce you to the benefits of the Mills & Boon® Book Club™—

- **FREE home delivery**
- **FREE gifts and competitions**
- **FREE monthly Newsletter**
- **Exclusive Mills & Boon Book Club offers**
- **Books available before they're in the shops**

Accepting these FREE books and gift places you under no obligation to buy, you may cancel at any time, even after receiving your free books. Simply complete your details below and return the entire page to the address below. You don't even need a stamp!

YES Please send me 2 free Modern books and a surprise gift. I understand that unless you hear from me, I will receive 4 superb new books every month for just £3.19 each, postage and packing free. I am under no obligation to purchase any books and may cancel my subscription at any time. The free books and gift will be mine to keep in any case.

Ms/Mrs/Miss/Mr_____ Initials _____

_____

Surname _____

Address _____

_____

_____ Postcode _____

Send this whole page to: Mills & Boon Book Club, Free Book Offer, FREEPOST NAT 10298, Richmond, TW9 1BR